A BRIEF FUTURE OF THE HUMAN RACE

A BRIEF FUTURE OF THE HUMAN RACE

Barry GJ Quinn

Copyright

Dedication

For Brian, Linda and David Quinn, *they were a family*

Table of Contents

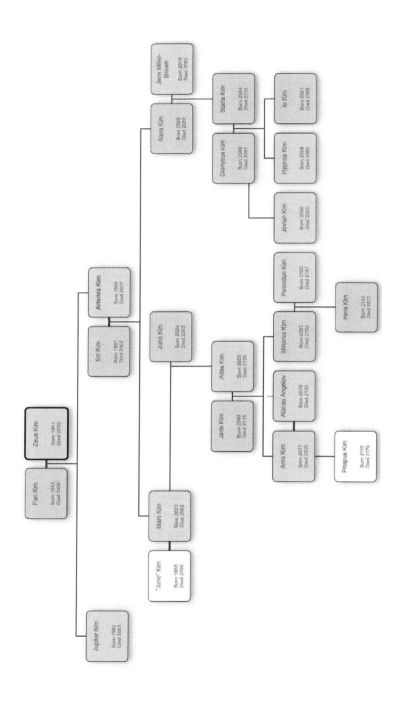

Introduction

This collection of short stories detail multiple generations of the Kim family. Some are astronauts and willingly go into space; others are forced when Earth becomes a ruin. Most of the stories in this collection are designed to be standalone with interwoven ideas connecting them, though some have been crafted specifically in order to link the narrative together.

A Brief Future of the Human Race originated in 2012; while developing story ideas as part of my Masters course in Creative Writing, I became fixated on the idea of a character being trapped, alone, in space. Written alongside a second, separate, story (both of which focused on deteriorating mental health), **The Abyss** was formed. Extensive research on Mars and space helped craft a more realistic story. Unknown to me at the time, I had just created the first Kim character: Alara.

Whilst designed as a standalone story, I wanted to know more about Alara and, chiefly, her daughter Starla. **Torn** was written next, which detailed a deteriorating Earth in which blame was, at least partially, attributed to Alara.

Next, I wanted to know about Alara's father, the figure that had inspired her to travel to Mars. Originally, Artemis had died as part of a test flight, something that was modified in redrafts in order to fit the overall narrative of the connected stories. **The Thirteenth Man on the Moon** introduces Artemis, whilst a throwaway line helped connect this story, and character, to a previously written and abandoned piece of flash-fiction, **Chips For Tea**.

I had the beginning of a family forming. I adapted previously written stories in order to fit into the growing narrative. Both **Isolate** and **Mimic (pt. I, II** and **III)** lent themselves nicely to the concept of Earth being rendered inhabitable and the search of a new home. **Isolate** explores the concept of identity, whilst the **Mimic** trilogy touches on mental health. Both stories were written, years prior, and were originally unconnected to the story of the Kims. It's as though, unconsciously, I was crafting a world in my head that, until I decided to weave together, were destined to remain separate.

13:30 served as a prequel to **The Abyss** and chartered Alara's initial exploration of space as part of an EVA, a concept I had wanted to explore for a while.

Other stories were crafted in order to link the narrative together: **They Were A Family,** which juxtaposes a domicile setting with the beginnings of first contact; **The Lightning-Struck Cubes, or: The Kinds**, which, originating as an abandoned narrative of flash-fiction, introduced a wider member of Alara's family and allowed me to explore a lot, chronologically, in only a few hundred words; **Child of the Rocket**, which explores an entire lifetime away from Earth, and touches on issues of sexuality and family, as well as helping bridge the gap between earlier and later stories; and **The Chronicles of Kim**, an insight into the future. *The Chronicles of Kim* was, for a long time, the title of this collection. Both **She** and **He**, originally separate entities from this collection, were added from pure vanity: I love them both.

Finally, **Since the Dawn of the Universe** and **The Narcissist**, both of which were written separately, were added to, almost, bookend the collection. Both stories are, I believe, brimming with hope and possibility, central themes to this collection.

Writing is a cathartic experience that helps me deal with issues in my own life. **I Would Give Everything, or: All The Things I Never Said** is a prime example. Ideas and concepts are all my own. If you read something that you like, make sure you let someone else know. And, make sure you let me know. Drop me a line on Twitter: @barrygjquinn_ or Instagram: barrygjquinn_author

I'd love to know what you thought.

Barry GJ Quinn
24/08/2019

Since the Dawn of the Universe

My affairs began some time ago, each burning bright and long. I saw nine souls over the course of my long life; or eight, depending on how you look at it. Some say I flirted with a tenth. Some souls were smooth, some rocky, some icy cold. Some were solid and some wispy. But all prevailed.

My first affair was with a man who blew hot and cold, depending upon his mood. Some days he held me in his warming embrace, whilst in others he angrily cocooned me in blistering coldness. He was bipolar in nature, with a craggy face and small stature. He was grey all over.

My second affair was with a golden goddess who masked her true feelings deep beneath the surface. I don't think I've ever seen her true inward guise. She was always warm, though, but extremely parched of love. With a slab-like face, she frequently spewed anger in burning eruptions meaning that our love was never without drama.

My third affair was with her twin, a multicoloured being brimming with life. She was the least toxic of my affairs, and purported longevity. She was emotional, though, crying oceans of tears that swamped our love. In parts dry, in parts cold, she had vast intelligence.

My fourth affair was with a sterile man who looked hot, but was icy beneath the surface. With a ruddy glow and an uneven face, he wasn't what many would call beautiful. But he was beautiful to me. Many have tried to discover his secrets, but he holds them close to his core.

My fifth affair was with a large-set man with a noticeable bulge around his mid region. But he is pretty to look at; in fact, he has 67 souls constantly trailing in his wake, mooning after his unrequited love. He has a hidden core of immense beauty, but masks it beneath many layers.

My sixth affair was with a yellowish man who wore many rings. He was nice to look at, too, but there was nothing beneath the outward veneer. But he was full of love. In fact, he radiated much more love for me than I gave him. Our affair wasn't healthy.

My seventh affair was with a ruler of many people, but the coldest of my many affections. He was featureless and bland. He was cold to the touch and, I suspect, cold inside too. He, too, wore many rings, though I fear this is the most interesting aspect of his personality.

My eighth affair was with his twin sister, a being with an uneven icy surface, but one which was cosmically more beautiful. But she keeps her distance from me, so much that her touch is one of the coldest in the known universe. She, too, was stormy in nature, and I could never be sure of her affection towards me. I'd like to think she was grateful for my love.

My ninth and final affair was with a small god whose status is now disputed. But I created him, and I nourished him through his teenage years. He follows me always, feeling little anger towards his demotion. He has a peculiar relationship with my eighth love.

My loves are long and my loves are burning. I hold them all in equal reverence. I think I love them all. I think they all love me. I give them life; they give me hope. They revolve around me. The universe revolves around me.

She

The clock strikes midnight, and her final day on Earth begins.

She carries out her daily routine. It is monotonous but necessary. First the makeup, then the wig, and afterwards the dress. The makeup emancipates the femininity within; the wig crowns her a woman. She's tried everything to hide *it*, but it hangs like a perpetual reminder of her wrongness. She's tucked it and taped it, but there it remains. Once she's in her dress everything seems to righten; the dress floats around her waist, helping to conceal her bulge. She's shaven her legs and wants to show them off. Why shouldn't she? She isn't harming anyone.

But nor is she fooling them.

Abuse is hurled. Screams of "faggot" and "fairy" and "freak" rent the air, crescendoing into oblivion. She is pushed and shoved and punched, but somehow she manages to keep her head held high. She has nothing to hide. This is her. She is no longer him.

The night is dark and cold. A billowing wind seems to push her onwards, and she clutches at her handbag. Inside is held her destiny. If she loses it, she loses herself.

She doesn't feel destined, though. She feels a fraud. She totters in her high heels, stumbling more than once. Her Adam's apple bulges. She has to readjust her stuffed bra. And all the while tears fall, relentless in their rivulets, trailing mascara down to her recently shaved jawline. She doesn't brush them aside. They have to see her pain, the torture she has endured.

She journeys through the labyrinthine maze of streets and alleyways until she arrives. She can see them far below, the cameraman and the boozing students, all rowdy and randy, oblivious to her plight.

She drops her bag and unloads her destiny.

She ties one end of the rope to the railing of the bridge as the icy wind blows at her wig, threatening to pull it away. She straightens herself out. She ties the other end of the rope into a noose, and slowly clambers up onto the railing. She's shaking, terrified of what is to come, but she knows it must happen. She cannot live like this. A year. That's what they said, the doctors and the psychologists. A year - she has to live as a woman for a year until she can truly become one. But she is one already; a year seems too long to righten her outward appearance. She's tired of the abuse, the loneliness of being herself. Alone, she can't cope. And she knows she'll always be alone. Her ravaged mind forgets her family.

Her present is bleak; her future is austere. She can't imagine a future for her.

So she takes her final bow. Head bent to the gathered drunkards below, she pulls the noose up and over her head. She tightens the strap and drops it. It hangs limply like a necklace. Then she unzips her dress and allows the front to drop. Her stuffed bra paints her feminine, but her stomach is naked to the wind as she shows the world her true self. She takes a step forward. Her stomach lurches; her heartbeat seems to stop.

She tilts over the edge and drops.

Flashes of life stream before her eyes. A baby. Her mother laughing. Her father shouting. A punch. A knife. The doctor's office. A bruise. A broken rib. Another punch. Her best friend's disgust. Him.

*

Her neck snaps from the jolt of the taut rope and she swings like a grotesque marionette's puppet. Below come the screams, the cries of terror. The camera swings up, forgetting the report of underage drinking, and zooms in on the woman hanging from the bridge. On her naked stomach is scrawled three words, three words she hopes will change the world.

"TRANSPHOBIA KILLED ME"

Chips For Tea

Chips for tea. With lots of vinegar.

I never thought I'd say that. Not up here. Not where we usually dine on protein packs and recycled urine. Not where food is limited, and vitamins are vital.

But tonight we're having chips. Made from fresh potatoes. Potatoes grown in space, of all places. Well, after lettuce, the only sensible follow up is potatoes. We can make lots from potatoes. Look at what your hard-earned British taxes are being put towards. Growing potatoes. In space! I think I'll call them space chips. That's a good name.

I've been given the job of dicing them up. I was a bit of a carpenter back at home - or, at least, I made my own furniture. From recycled scrap. Basically I reupholstered them, but a carpenter sounds so much better than a reupholster, right? That's what I tell myself, anyway. And that's what I tell others, too. So naturally I've been deemed as the most proficient carver. I don't know where they get that idea from. Maybe it's because I can cut wood with extreme precision. But apparently that means I can cut the chips perfectly, without wasting any of the potatoes. We're having them with skins on. We're not wasting any of these babies.

The vinegar was sent up with us. Your taxes paid for that, too. We can't make vinegar from scratch in space, unfortunately.

I'm used to looking out at a sweeping view of London skyscrapers when I'm preparing dinner at home. Now I'm looking at a glorious view of Earth, turning majestically in the sun-soaked abyss of space. Auroral lights splay in dazzling serenity and the cosmos comes alive in a charge of colour - red, blue, black, orange - but all of this pales in comparison. All I can think about is chips for tea.

We've waited three years for this.

Cooked in a slow-fryer using extreme heat, the chips come out limp, brown, dry and brittle. But after dining on protein packs for 1,095 days, they taste like heaven. Extremely vinegary heaven.

The Thirteenth Man on the Moon

The footprints remained untarnished.

They were large - a nine, or maybe a ten. Possibly even an eleven. They trailed in arcs around the landing site, indicating where Armstrong and Aldrin had stepped years previously.

That's one small step for a man, one giant leap for mankind.

Artemis Kim tried to imagine what the two astronauts had felt upon stepping on the surface of the moon. Armstrong, in particular, must have felt a sense of pride. He was the first man, after all. Aldrin had, and would, go down in history, too. And yet history would always remember him as the *second.*

How many have there been since?

He couldn't quite remember. He made a mental note to ask Gowland later - in private, of course. He should be clued up on such knowledge. He'd become a laughing stock if it became known that he couldn't remember his heritage.

Artemis pressed on.

Behind him, he heard Gowland breathing shallowly.

Okay, so he didn't actually hear her *behind* him, but he could hear her breathing issuing through their shared comm, and he knew that Gowland was behind him, so technically he *was* right. Gowland was the... something person on the moon, but she had an even greater accolade to add to that. She was the first *woman* on the moon. She would go down in history - even more so than Artemis.

55 years had passed since the last man - Harrison Schmitt - had spent almost an entire day on the luna surface. Many were questioning why money was being wasted on sending a new batch of astronauts up but they didn't know the truth. They couldn't know the truth.

Artemis turned - slowly, for there was no atmosphere - and gave Gowland a thumbs up. She returned it a moment later.

"Almost there," he said through their shared comm. It was shared between only them, Azad back on the command and service module in orbit, and Nelson and Rivera back in Cumbria. No one else was allowed to listen in. No one else was allowed to know.

He passed long-abandoned equipment and scraps of rubbish sent up in '69, deposited not far from the flag. The great American flag. It had toppled over - some thought when *Eagle* had blasted from the surface, others thought it was time itself - faded to white, and eroded considerably. White.

Surrender.

Artemis hoped this notion wouldn't come to fruition.

Careful not to step in Armstrong's footfalls, Artemis stopped and peered down at the white flag. In actual fact it was mere scraps of fabric now, but the importance of the act still sat strongly within him. An American flag. On the moon. Today they would leave the first British flag, alongside the Afghanistan flag, a token to represent Azad's involvement in the mission. Both Artemis and Gowland were English born and bred, but Azad had resided in Afghanistan for the first few years of his life.

Artemis wanted to bend and touch the flag, but thought better of it. Such an act would be seen as sacrilege amongst those watching back at home. Though the true meaning of their mission was secret, the world at large knew that they had been sent to the moon. They could hardly keep it secret; the English Space Agency had been very vocal in promoting England joining the space race.

Instead, Artemis simply stood for a moment and basked in the history of the first moon landing. He though of Aldrin, nearing his 98th birthday, and of Collins and Armstrong. Did they realise, back in '69, that their mission would have such a legacy? What would be the legacy of Artemis' mission?

Gowland fell inline beside him, and the two astronauts stood in silence, both looking down at the flag.

"Seems a long time since those chips, eh," Gowland said, chuckling.

"Hmm? Yeah. Can still taste the vinegar."

Gowland patted Artemis on the shoulder. "What should we do first?" she asked. "The flags, or the photo?"

Artemis shrugged. "Don't mind."

"You okay?" Gowland was readying the selfie stick.

"Yeah."

"You've gone a bit quiet."

"Just thinkin'."

"No bother, no bother."

Back in '69 many had proclaimed Apollo 11 as a suicide mission due to the vast amount of unknowables related to their mission. Ever since Artemis had signed up to the English Space Agency missions - the Quirinus programme - he had had a niggling doubt that he had signed up for his own suicide. Especially with—

"Ready?" Gowland cut into his thoughts. She held the selfie stick before them both.

"Should we be doing that here?" Artemis asked, looking up from the flag at his feet.

"Sure, why not?"

"This is where Apollo 11 landed."

"It's also where Quirinus 3 landed," Gowland countered.

"Touché," Artemis said. He stepped to Gowland and raised his fingers into a peace sign near his helmet. Gowland did the same, and then she snapped several selfies, documenting their arrival on the luna surface.

As Gowland busied herself with checking how the photos looked, Artemis pulled the two flags from his belt. He turned to look at the half-Earth, visible over distant craters. It really was quite incredible, a sight that he would never tire of looking upon. Earth appeared alone, untarnished by stars or the white sun, which was currently situated somewhere to Artemis' right. He thought of his home, of his family and his children. Sol would be currently watching his movements from the English Space Agency headquarters in Cumbria, with Alara and Mars probably squabbling at her feet, unable to comprehend the magnitude of what they were watching on the television screens. They were too young to understand that their daddy was an astronaut; to them, the figure presented on the screen would most likely be just another character from one of their favourite shows.

Artemis separated the two flags. It was time for him to say something monumental, to go down in history alongside Armstrong.

He placed the Afghanistan flag at his feet and raised the English one aloft. It stood stationary in the almost vacuum, unnerving Artemis slightly. But he didn't voice his disquietude. Gowland began snapping photos; he could hear her murmuring over their private comm.

"It has been 55 years since man last stepped on the surface of the moon," Artemis said into the collective comm system, the one that was patched into the entirety of the English Space Agency. He had rehearsed the words countless times. He hadn't written them himself. "Today, on the fifth of March, 2027, we are back. We have completed our goal of landing the first woman and the next man on the moon. Today we have taken that next small step that will lead to the giant leap to Mars."

Artemis switched from the collective comm as soon as he had finished the rehearsed words, not wanting to hear the congratulations from the planet below. He didn't like the fact that the words they had forced him to speak harkened so significantly back to those spoken 58 years previously by Armstrong. He also didn't want to hear Sol or his children, feeling they would distract him from the mission at hand.

He pushed the flag into the surface of the moon. The sharp dust proved, once more, troublesome, and he had to exert more pressure than would have been needed on Earth. He remembered hearing that Armstrong and Aldrin had managed to get their flag about seven inches deep, and Artemis wanted to best them. He pushed and pushed, feeling the shaft travelling slowly into the luna surface.

Eventually he gave up. He studied the pole and estimated that around seven inches were buried beneath his feet. *Possibly closer to eight,* he thought. The ghost of a smug smile stretched across his thin face.

He then repeated the act with the second flag. The black, red and green stripes would fade quickly, meaning that the two flags would be indistinguishable before long. Just how they should be.

Equal.

"I got some good photos," Gowland said, thrusting her camera into Artemis' face. He glanced down as she scrolled. One of the photos showed him from the back, with both flags standing stationary at either side of his bulky suit. In the forefront was Earth, blue and white and beautiful.

"That's the one," he said. "My kids will see that one." He smiled behind his visor, before looking up at Gowland. "Want me to take some of you?"

"Would you? Please!" Gowland passed him the camera and Artemis took a few dozen photos of her around the flags, with the remnants of Apollo 11 in the background. He then took a few of the surface of the moon. In reality they would look identical in their suits. They were similar of height. Most likely, no one back home would be able to tell them apart. But they knew. And now they both had photographic proof that they had been here... until the conspiracy theorists tried to argue otherwise.

Artemis checked the time on the readout on his wrist. Right now someone from the English Space Agency would be telling reporters from all across the world that Artemis and Gowland would be beginning their task of collecting rock samples and drilling beneath the surface, but that was what the rovers were for. Artemis and Gowland had a second mission to complete.

"Just to confirm," Azad said through their earpieces, "you are now completely disengaged from the collective comm system. We're free to talk about the mission."

Artemis craned his neck. Well, in actual fact he had to lean backwards so that his head moved upwards - *damn these suits are bulky.* Directly above their head, midway through its orbit around the moon, their multi-purpose crew vehicle floated. It was too far for Artemis to see the windows, but he liked to imagine that Azad was looking down at them.

"How far from the coordinates?" Artemis asked.

"About 550 meters," Azad replied. "From your current location head towards the Apollo 11 landing site; it's past there."

Artemis knew that Azad had trackers of their two suits and was reading their location from the screens in front of him. They were one of the failsafes that the English Space Agency had demanded.

"It shouldn't take too long," Gowland said. "No need for the buggy."

"You sure?" Artemis asked.

"This is probably the only time in our life that we'll be able to *walk* on the moon, Kim. Come on, let's hop."

And so they began. Bunny hops on the moon, Artemis conceded, were quite fun. The lack of atmosphere meant that they had to be careful where they placed their feet, but otherwise it was an enjoyable journey. Earth was to their right, and as much as Artemis would have liked to feed on the view he knew such recklessness would probably lead to an injury, and so his eyes feasted upon the shores and rocks before him. Their destination was West, a small crater in Mare Tranquillitatis, otherwise known as the Sea of Tranquility. It was here that the signal had originated.

A small part of Artemis still thought the signal had come from some piece of equipment left behind from the previous missions, but the rational part of his mind argued otherwise. How would the equipment - whatever it was - get to West? Only one other team had landed at Tranquility Base, and the furthest Armstrong had ventured was Little West, a small crater around 60 meters from their landing site. No atmosphere meant no wind. There was no feasible way that a piece of equipment left behind by Armstrong and Aldrin could have travelled nearly 500 meters on the surface of the moon by itself. And, it was unlikely that it would still be operational after so much time.

The signal had to come from something else.

An even smaller part of him thought that Russia or China had landed a team near West in secret, but again his rational mind had an argument ready. There was no way they could have done so in secret. The moon had eyes on it at all times; even if a lander had been launched in secret, someone would have seen it arrive in orbit.

So where was the signal coming from?

Artemis had his suspicions, as did Gowland and Azad and Nelson and Rivera. For some reason no one had yet voiced them. Artemis knew they were all thinking the same thing.

Artemis lost track of time as they jumped across the lunar surface, but before long the rim of the crater loomed up dark and foreboding. The signal originated from within, near the far shore. As they reached the edge of West, Artemis saw that most of the crater was smothered in darkness. The white sun gleamed before them, basking West in shadows.

"Are you creeped out?" Artemis asked. "Because I am."

"Not at all," Gowland said, a chuckle in her voice.

"Hmm."

"Why are you?"

"Look at it," Artemis said, pointing for added effect. "It's pitch black. We can't see a thing."

"Look at where we are," Gowland argued. "We're on the moon. Did you really think it would be that straightforward?"

"I guess not."

"So - are we walking around? Or down and through?"

"Why are you asking me?"

"Well, uh… You're the Commander."

"Oh."

Artemis considered the two options. Walking around would take longer, but it also meant they would be able to look down the crater and into the shadows to see what lay within. Directly entering West, and hopping across, would half the time.

"I say we go into the crater. It's not that deep," Gowland said. "We'll be able to get out easily if we need to."

"Why would we need to?" Artemis asked.

Gowland didn't answer. She didn't need to.

"Okay," he finally said. "We'll go in."

"Remember," Nelson said, "you're only to ascertain the source of the signal. It's most likely originating from a secret mission from China or something, but I want you both to be careful. And make sure your video feeds are on."

Artemis had forgotten all about Nelson and Rivera; it was the first either had spoken in quite some time. But he did as he was instructed, and switched the cameras on, one each side of his visor.

As Commander, Artemis took the first leap. He jumped down into the crater, skidding slightly on the uneven terrain. His knees almost buckled, but he managed to remain upright.

"Careful," he said to Gowland who, a moment later, joined him in West. She landed much more gracefully.

West was around the size of a football field; it wouldn't take them long to cross it. Regardless, they journeyed slowly. Artemis could hear Gowland's breathing through their comm and he wondered whether she was as scared as he was. He didn't dare ask her over the comm. He shelved that alongside his previous question.

As they hopped in silence he racked his brains, trying to figure it out.

Armstrong and Aldrin landed on July 21, 1969, and Conrad and Bean landed four months later. The next landing wasn't until '71, and it included Shephard and... and... Artemis couldn't remember his name, but there had been two in that mission, so that was 6. The last mission was in '72, bringing the total to 8.

Artemis cut to the comm shared between only him and Gowland.

"Hey, Gowland, humour me a moment. Back in '72 - was there just the one mission to the moon, or two?"

"Two." Gowland looked over at Artemis. "Why?"

Two. That made 10. Was he the eleventh man on the moon then?

"Just trying to work something out."

They reached the shadows. Artemis took the first jump into them.

"Young and Duke went up in April, and then Cernan and Schmitt went in December."

"You've got a good memory," Artemis said.

"Why do you ask?"

They fell into darkness. The lights from their helmets penetrated only a little; they could see just beyond the reach of their footballs, but nothing else. They should have brought more powerful torches. *Hindsight is a wonderful thing.*

"Just trying to remember all those that came before us. I've got Armstrong and Aldrin, Conrad and Bean and Shephard, plus the four you just mentioned. Who came up with Shephard?"

"Edgar Mitchell," Gowland replied. "Stuart Roosa stayed in the Command Module."

"Mitchell, of course."

"Then there was Scott and Irwin, in '71."

"Which makes... 12. 12 men have been here before us."

"Yeah. I'm the first woman on the moon. You're the thirteenth man."

The thirteenth man. The thirteenth man on the moon.

Artemis wasn't a superstitious man, but he didn't like the idea of him being the thirteenth man.

"Not long now," Azad said.

"What can you see?" Rivera asked.

"Not much," Artemis replied. "It's pitch-black. Can barely see in front of us."

"No signs that anyone has been there? No footsteps? No debris?"

"No, nothing." Artemis swept his face left to right; his torches shone on the surface, illuminating rocks and dust, tiny pockmarks within the crater.

"It should be just up ahead," Azad said.

"Are you still receiving us?" Gowland asked.

"Loud and clear," Nelson replied.

Artemis counted the remaining steps. *One, two, three.* He glanced over at Gowland. *Four, five, six.* He looked ahead. *Seven, eight, nine.* Still nothing. *Ten, eleven, twelve.* Wait - was that… *Thirteen—*

He stopped walking. Gowland stopped to his left.

*

"We *have* to say he returned," Nelson said to Sol Kim. He spoke passionately, but Sol could tell that he was extremely agitated. Worried about the shit-storm that was hovering over him, ready to drop at any moment.

"But he didn't," Sol replied quietly. She thought of Alara and Mars, both of whom would never see their father again. *A child should never have to endure that,* she thought. She wanted to cry, but she was all cried out. She just felt empty. How on earth was she supposed to tell her children that their father was dead?

"Gowland will take the truth to her grave, as will I, James Rivera, and Azad. We need you to sign the same document. We'll tell the world that Kim returned alongside Gowland and then stage a car crash en route to you and your children."

Sol noted that Nelson had referred to her husband as *Kim*. She wanted to slap him, to scream Artemis' name into his face.

"We hope that the shock of him not reuniting with you and your children will detract from the truth. We have the backing of the Prime Minister and his entire administration. They all think this is the best scenario." Nelson looked at Sol with sympathy, but she knew he didn't feel it. He was more worried about saving his own ass.

"To lie? To the world? To my children? I can't lie to them, I can't lie for the rest of my life."

"You have to."

"I *have* to?"

"Yes."

"Why? What really happened up there? What happened that meant my husband died, but Joanie Gowland lived?"

"Your husband sacrificed his life so that Gowland would live. He managed to help Gowland return to the module but he didn't manage to enter alongside her. He told her to launch without him."

"So he's still up there? All alone?" Still the tears refused to come.

"No. He's dead. Gowland saw him die as she rose from the surface."

"How? How did he die? If you want me to sign that damn piece of paper and lie to my children for the rest of my life - tell me the truth!" Anger burst from Sol with such force that Nelson was momentarily take aback.

He composed himself for a moment and smoothed down his tie.

"At 17.26, UTC, Commander Artemis Kim was killed by an unknown and unidentified entity on the lunar surface."

The words washed over Sol, but she didn't understand. "An unknown... and unidentified... what... I don't..."

"An alien. We believe an alien killed your husband."

13:30

Alara Kim popped her contacts in and the world's news was beamed across her vision. The headlines read as thus: famine was steadily sweeping across Eastern Europe; President Baldwin was to remain in office for a second term; and Lady Gaga had announced the release of her tenth album. No word on the English Space Agency, or the astronauts preparing for their latest mission. Interest was wavering.

Alara blinked three times in rapid sequence and the feed changed. Her emails popped up. The usual junk. Glancing downwards, the feed scrolled down slowly and a solitary word caught her attention. Home.

She widened her eyes and the feed zoomed in on the email. One blink opened it.

Over her vision of a clouded Earth, Alara Kim read the email from her mother.

"Alara,

You are doing so well. The world is watching you, and I am praying for your safe journey to Mars. I am so proud of you, and I'm sure your father would be too.

Starla misses her mum. I miss you too. She's always asks when she can see you. I haven't yet told her that you won't be coming home. I don't know how to. But I keep telling her that you'll be back soon. What about a video call? Would that be possible? It's been so long since our last, and I know it would do Starla a world of good. She's talking in full sentences now. So much has changed since your last call.

I hope you're doing okay. I know you are, but I still like to hear it directly from you, rather than hearing it on the news. *It's hard having you away from home, but you are doing yourself so proud. You'll be remembered, that's for sure. Two astronauts in one family. Who else can say that?*

Hoping to hear from you soon.
Love always,
Mum."

Alara blinked back tears and winked her left eye once. Her contact lenses opened the 'reply' tab. She spoke her response aloud, and the lenses automatically typed it out.

"Mum,

Thanks for the email. I'm doing fine up here. I wish you could see it. I'm taking plenty of pictures; I'll attach a few for you to look through. I've got my first spacewalk later and surprisingly I'm not scared. I've been told it'll be exactly like the extravehicular activity (EVA) simulators.

I'll ask about a video call, but I can't promise anything. They like the limit that sort of thing to stop us getting homesick. I may be able to call, though. I'll ask and let you know. I miss Starla so much. It's hard knowing she's so close, and yet so far. I think of her every moment I'm awake, and I dream of her too. Keep telling her to look for the brightest star, Mum. Keep telling her to look for me.

Hope you're well.
Love,
Alara."

Alara winked her left eye again and a series of photos were displayed. She looked left; the photos scrolled. She winked her left eye over the three most recent photographs, and they were attached to the email. Winking once more, the email was sent.

Closing down her emails, Alara's photos remained on her lenses. Looking left, she scrolled through photos of her daughter. Alara had left Earth shortly after Starla's first birthday, and she had changed so much in the intervening year. Chubby of face, black of hair, Starla Kim was a little over two years of age and, so Alara had been repeatedly told, the double of Alara herself. Alara couldn't see it; or rather she refused to see it, for every time she looked at herself in the mirror she saw her daughter staring back, and the thought of never seeing her again almost made her want to abandon her lifelong dream and return to Earth.

She wouldn't ask about video calls or phone calls. She didn't want to speak to her daughter. She knew she wouldn't be able to maintain her strength if she heard her daughter's voice, a voice she'd never heard before. She didn't want to taunt herself with impossibilities.

She winked her right eye now. The feed faded. The lenses became clear.

Below the Earth shimmered intoxicatingly, and for a moment Alara simply bathed in its serenity. Blues and oranges and greens and whites - simple colours that reminded her of home. It was nighttime in England; she could tell from the angle of the moon. Her daughter would be sleeping now.

Tears surged to her eyes as she looked at the moon. She'd always had a morbid fascination with the moon. She found it beautiful. It was grey and vague and paled in comparison to Earth, but to Alara it was much more captivating. She surmised this was why she wanted to colonise Mars: it, too, was barren, sterile. If Alara was sterile, she wouldn't have Starla missing her on Earth. If Alara was sterile, she wouldn't be missing her daughter who she'd never see again.

"Alara."

A voice from behind. Alara blinked away her tears and turned to find Nadia Hassan approaching her. She looked worried.

"Are you ready? We have to put our suits on soon."

Alara cleared her throat. "Yeah, just finished breakfast," she replied. She looked down at her plate. "I'll clean up later."

"Tom wants us suited up by eleven," Nadia said. "We walk at one."

"Sure thing."

Alara followed Nadia.

*

The airlock was pressurised. As were their suits.

Everything was primed.

"Are you ready?" Tom asked over the intercom.

Alara gave him a thumbs-up. Nadia nodded her domed head.

"Commencing countdown. May God's love be with you."

Alara Kim readied herself.

"Ten."

Her heart thumped like an African drum incessantly beating out a never-ending tune of trepidation. It thumped dully in-line with Tom's countdown.

"Nine."

She looked to Nadia. Nadia looked to her.

"Eight."

Both astronauts nodded.

"Seven."

Alara raised his arm. It seemed to take an age to lift. She gripped the wall-mounted railing as though her very life depended on it. In some ways it did.

"Six."

Earth swam below them, a multicoloured ball of normalcy. She saw it through the circular windows of the door before them.

"Five."

Alara swallowed hard. Her head wavered from the influx of pure oxygen. This was what she had trained all her life for. This moment. Right here.

"Four."

The engines of the space station stuttered and came to a complete standstill. All unnecessary equipment was cut off. Everything was primed.

"Three."

She looked from Earth to the moon, and a smile attached itself to her face.

"Two."

A calming sense of clarity overcame Alara suddenly. It was as though she and the Earth below were as one; she sensed she could feel the minuscule movements of her home planet; could feel the anticipation of every soul below as they awaited her disembarking.

"One."

The airlock hissed slowly open. She didn't hear a sound.

Alara floated from the airlock. The tether connecting her to the space station unravelled like a coiled snake behind her as she drifted out into space.

It was quite like swimming; certainly it felt no different than the practice runs they had endured in the Neutral Buoyancy Laboratory near the Scottish border. That pool held 4 billion gallons of water, and now Alara knew exactly why so much water had been part of their EVA training.

As if to test the similarities, Alara drew her arms before her in a breaststroke formation, and her body tumbled forward, floating steadily. She couldn't help herself; she laughed aloud. *Oh, if you could see me now, Dad*, she thought, her gaze flicking to the huge ball of life beneath her. Her father was buried there, somewhere. She couldn't see much of England, and what little she could see was wreathed in clouds.

She 'swam' again, drawing further away from the station, enjoying the simplicity of her movements, the serenity of the silence that swathed her.

"This is…" she began, but cut herself off. Words failed her.

"The satellite's over here," came Nadia's voice, converted from sound wave into speech by Alara's headset. It took a few seconds for her to understand what she was saying.

Using her SAVER (Supplied Air for EVA Rescue), Alara blasted to the left, rocketing around the station. The jet thruster in her backpack propelled her after Nadia. Her tools, tethered to her, trailed in her wake.

Tethered to the space station, Alara swung around in a majestic arc and fell beside the broken satellite. Nadia had already begun work.

"The solar panels aren't connecting," she explained once Alara steadied herself.

Alara gripped onto the side of the station, trying her hardest to keep her heart rate steady. The excitement of being out in space flooded her, threatening to floor her and she knew it would do no good to lose herself given her present predicament. Given what was to come. Given what she had to do.

"Any idea what happened?" Alara asked, trying to keep her voice steady.

A moment later, once her headset had translated the sound waves, Nadia replied: "Probably just too much energy feeding into it from the sun. Maybe some debris from a meteoroid hitting it. Doesn't matter." She shrugged her shoulders, causing her bulky suit to shift awkwardly. "It'll be easily rectified, I hope. Open the schematics."

Neither astronaut voiced what both knew the other was thinking. Their words were being recorded, and no official confirmation of their true mission must be documented. But Alara looked to Nadia, who minutely nodded her head. The great domed helmet caused the entire spacesuit to shift slightly.

Alara blinked rapidly thrice, and her contact lenses activated. In the top corner the time read 13:05. She blinked once more, followed by three left winks, a right wink, and two further blinks. The schematics of the satellite opened before her. Tilting her head, they fell inline with the satellite in front of them, and she understood exactly where everything was.

"I'm going to start off by changing the connecting wires," Nadia said. "Hopefully it'll be as simple as that."

"What do you want me to do?" Alara asked, trying to keep her head steady so that the schematics stayed in place.

"Unscrew the panelling - make sure you grab the screws before they float away! I'll strip the wiring ready to be replaced."

Alara nodded her head, before realising that Nadia wasn't looking at her. So she said: "Sure thing," and leant towards the solar panelling that spread across the entire surface of the station. "It's just the few panels around the satellite, right?"

"Right."

Alara nodded her head again, before reaching back to draw in the floating tools that bobbed around her like apples in a barrel. She fished around for the screwdriver and began her work of removing the solar panels. As she worked she watched the clock ticking towards half one. Towards...

Absently, Alara found she had already removed one panel, doing so autonomously. One screw had evaded her, but she'd managed to catch the others. It was, to her, rather like trying to catch a buzzing fly. Almost impossible when focused, but strangely possible when vacant of mind. It didn't really matter either way as she had spares, but the less equipment they sent spiralling into space the better.

Alara scrambled over to the neighbouring panel and began removing it. The first screw darted away like a fish. She stretched out after it, but it was drawn away much too quickly for her to catch. She swore beneath her breath.

She found her mind wavered a lot as she worked. The work itself was banal, everyday. But she found her eyes trawling the abyss of space around them as though she was desperate to take in every sight. She snapped her eyes in rapid sequence, and a stream of photographs were taken.

First she took a photo of the stretch of space before her, with stars winking all around. She looked to the largest, and imagined it was this which her daughter would look to when seeking sanctuary about her absent mother: she'd told her daughter, and her mother to remind her daughter, that the largest star in the night sky would be Alara looking down at her. Next she took several photos of their work on the satellite, knowing that the English Space Agency would want such documentation. From here she captured the planet, zooming in on certain countries by widening her eyes. She snapped the Great Wall of China, the Pyramids of Giza, and the remains of the Amazon rainforest. Her contacts were sophisticated, capable of zooming in with precision.

And as if drawn like a gigantic magnet, Alara found her eyes locking on the cratered moon, and she took dozens of photos. The natural satellite was really rather remarkable, and it was most definitely beautiful. Pale shades of grey married with creams and whites to produce something equally, if not more, captivating than the planet it circled. Alara found it hard to draw her eyes away, and she lost another two screws to space.

"Alara, focus," said Nadia.

Alara shook her head and returned to the task at hand. "Sorry," she said. She removed the second panel and tied it to a free tether, before moving to the third and final board. She positioned the schematics. This one she removed more quickly, and she managed to catch each of the eight screws. She pushed them into a floating bag, and tied up the panel. It floated slowly up.

The stripped wire danced around Nadia's head as she bent to the satellite and pulled the original from its connection points. With deft agility Nadia snatched at it before it managed to float away, and she pushed it into the floating bag.

"You've had more practice at this," murmured Alara.

"Course I have; this is my third spacewalk, my third time fixing something broken. You'll get the hang of it before long."

Alara looked to the time. 13:20.

Nadia connected the fresh wiring. Without the central solar panels, which were in turn connected to every other panel, there was nothing to hook up the satellite with the solar power. "Put one of the panels back in place," said Nadia. "No need to screw it in just yet. I only need to see if it's powering the satellite or not. If not… well, it's gonna require some further investigation. We may have to pull this baby to pieces."

Alara pulled in the nearest panel and pushed it back into place. Power sparked for the briefest of moments, before cutting off just as quickly. Nadia groaned aloud.

"What?" asked Alara, confused. "What? What does that mean?"

"I'm not entirely sure," replied Nadia. "Could just be a dodgy panel, maybe. Hopefully. We brought a spare, right?"

"Yeah. It's here, somewhere." Alara scrambled around for the treasures that trailed her. Screwdrivers, pliers, bags of nuts and bolts, hammers, wires, circuit boards. Everything they may possibly need to fix a fault on the space station.

She found the new solar panel floating to her left. Behind it the moon winked alluringly.

She stripped it of its packaging and pushed it into place. Power surged into the satellite as it whirred into life.

"Yes!" Nadia hissed.

"What?" Alara asked. "Is that it? Does that mean it's working?"

"Yes, I think so."

Along the side of the space station little lights sparked into being, indicating that each of the solar panels were now connected to the mainframe.

"Quick, screw it into place," said Alara. "Quick, before I lose it."

Nadia stretched for the floating bag and screwdriver, and began screwing the panel back in place. As she did, Alara looked to the time. 13:24.

"We've only been out here twenty four minutes," Alara said, alerting Nadia to the time.

"I was hoping it wouldn't take long," Nadia replied. She began to screw the second panel into place, which Alara held for her. "Now we'll be able to spend more time experimenting. We have three hours put aside for this walk."

"May as well make the most of it," finished Alara with a knowing smile.

Alara and Nadia moved to the third and final panel. Alara held it in place and watched Nadia screw it back.

"Tom," Nadia said once it was firmly held in place. "How's everything looking your end?"

A moments pause. Then: "Everything's looking great. Good job guys."

"I think that's everything then," said Nadia.

"Before we start the experiments we need to take a selfie," said Alara.

Since Tim Peake's historic viral photo in 2016 it had become tradition for astronauts to capture their time out in space with a selfie, and Alara was keen to join the growing legacy. She stretched out for the floating camera stick and held it out in front of her helmeted face. Reflected in the dome Alara saw Nadia present a peace sign with her right hand, whilst gripping onto the station with her left. Alara herself hooked one of her legs around a handrail so she didn't float away. It was now 13:26.

She zoomed out slightly, so that Earth below was also reflected and, much to her delight, so was the moon. She snapped the capture button several times.

"Oh, yeah," she said, grinning at the surrealism of taking a selfie in space. She let the camera float away, before its tether tightened and it bobbed back. "I'll upload it when we get back inside."

"I almost forgot about that," said Nadia.

"So did I," replied Alara. 13:28.

"Right, well, it's time to start work. Come on, over here. Tom," she added as an afterthought. "Let us know if you experience any more power fluctuations. I think everything's alright, but you can never be too careful."

"Will do," replied Tom. "I'll let you guys know when it's time to return."

"Okay," said Nadia, before turning to Alara. "Right, this way."

Nadia led Alara over to the far side of the station, using handrails to crawl along its surface. Alara followed. Nadia stopped with Earth behind them; it was now 13:29.

"We have just over two and a half hours," Alara said in a thin voice, once more alerting Nadia to the time. A minute nod told Alara that Nadia had understood her meaning.

"Right, well, what we have to do is—"

As Nadia spoke, Alara reached for the next handrail to pull herself closer. Her hand slipped and she fell forward, smashing her helmet off of the surface of the station. As she fell, she automatically released her left hand from its grasp to try and prevent her fall, realising as she did so that there was now nothing keeping her connected to the station except her tether.

She scrambled for purchase, but too late.

She began to float away from the space station, and towards Earth. It was now 13:30.

"Alara!" Nadia cried out, reaching for her.

Alara stretched out her hand; their fingers connected for the briefest of moments, glove-upon-glove, but they had little grip. Her stretched fingers slipped from Nadia's curled digits, and she fell away.

She was falling fast, and she watched in horror as her tether tightened and stretched. It reached its full elasticity and held for a moment, and Alara bobbed up and down. She reached out for the tether, scrambling to gain purchase, to righten herself, and began to pull.

The tether snapped.

Immediately Alara began to tumble away from the station. She span around and faced Earth as she fell towards it.

"Alara! Alara! Tom, Alara's tether snapped. She's falling. She's..."

Nadia's voice faded to nothingness as Alara fell further away.

For an unfathomable amount of time Alara let herself fall. It was almost as though she didn't believe it was happening; or rather, she refused to believe it. But as her eyes snapped to the moon the seriousness of her predicament fell over her, and Alara finally released a pent-up scream. It penetrated her dome, swelling deafeningly. And that was when she realised her helmet had a crack in its outer layer.

Panic set in. Her training hadn't covered this.

Momentum picked up. She continued to spin, increasing in speed, falling further away from the station and safety, and closer towards an unavoidable death.

"Alara!"

A voice spoke, and it took Alara a moment to recognise it.

"Tom! Tom!" she gasped out. "Tom, I'm falling. I... I... What do I do?"

"Your SAVER!" cried Tom. "Use your SAVER."

It took Alara a few seconds to realise what Tom was talking about. Then she scrambled around for the joystick. She pressed a button at random, and the thruster in the centre of her backpack burst, blasting her forward. She'd pressed the wrong one.

All sanity was failing her. Upon each rotation she looked towards the moon, finding it hard, despite her predicament, to look anywhere else.

"Alara! Your SAVER."

"I know, I know, I'm trying," she cried back, wailing almost. "It didn't work. It didn't work."

"You have to slow down. Only then will you have any control."

"How? How do I slow down?"

"Use the top and bottom blasters at the same time. That should level things out."

Alara did as she was instructed, and pressed both buttons simultaneously. Immediately it had an impact. Her fall was stalled, and she juddered slowly, bouncing all the while. She was still falling towards Earth, but her descent was much slower now.

"Keep doing that," said Tom. "Keep them both pressed. You have to slow down."

Her fingers ached from pressing the joystick, but Alara refused to let go. This was her only chance at surviving.

Eventually her speed levelled out. Eventually she stopped, floating steadily in space. She was no longer rotating. She took a moment to compose herself, to try and regain control over her breathing.

"I'm—" she gasped. "I'm—I've stopped. Stopped. I've..."

"Are you okay?" Tom asked. Alara could hear the worry in his voice.

"I'm..." She trailed off as her eyes once more sought the moon, as though a magnetic attraction connected them. She nodded her head. "Yes. I'm fine."

"You're not that far from the station," said Tom hurriedly. "You should be able to fly back with the SAVER. Don't worry - I'll be here every step of the way. Head back for Nadia. She'll help you back inside. Damn, this never should have happened!"

"It's alright," said Alara, speaking not to Tom but rather the distant moon below. "It's alright. I'm alright. I'm fine."

"Use the SAVER," prompted Tom. "Come on, get back here."

Alara could tell he was thinking of the storm inevitably brewing below; was thinking of the anger her accident would induce in the people of Earth. People would claim her job was no longer safe, but Alara would laugh at such suggestions. Of course being an astronaut wasn't safe! It never had been.

Slowly, her hand shaking, Alara took hold of the joystick and turned it; immediately her body twisted around and she faced the space station again. Her heartbeat levelled out at the sight of it. It wasn't that far - Tom was right. Only a few meters, really. And even less, what with Nadia reaching for her, dangling on the end of her tether.

Only a few metres.

She told herself over and over as she initiated the return journey. The SAVER blasted her forward and though she was desperate to return to safety, she forced herself not to go too fast. She may misjudge her destination, and may miss Nadia and the station all together, and she didn't think she'd be able to keep ahold of her sanity long enough to attempt it again. If she missed, she'd die. It was a simple as that.

Her fall from the station had felt like mere seconds; the return felt like hours.

But eventually she made it. Stretching out her free shaking hand, Alara grabbed hold of Nadia's hand and clung to it desperately. She was all too aware that her grasp was painfully tight, but she didn't care.

"Get me back to the station," she gasped. "Please."

"Hey, you're alright," said Nadia. "Try and keep calm. You're alright." She turned back to the station. "Grab onto my waist or leg - I'll need both of my arms to pull us back in."

Alara did as Nadia had instructed, and gripped onto her waist as Nadia began to pull them both back in towards the space station. It was strenuous going, and very slow, but Alara guessed Nadia felt likewise - she didn't want to go too fast, lest her tether snapped too. If it did, they'd both be goners.

Eventually they arrived back at the station, and both shaking women crawled back to the airlock using the handrails. Alara had no idea how she managed to stand upright as the airlock depressurised; once it was done, and the opposite door opened to the station, she crumbled to the floor. She cried.

*

"That was a close call! All is fine. Next leap, Mars…"

Alara captioned the selfie and uploaded it to Twitter.

*

In next to no time the selfie went viral. It was shared alongside numerous news reports of her almost death. Alara read them on her lenses: some did indeed warn of the dangers of sending astronauts into space. Others labelled Alara as the greatest astronaut ever. But one thing was clear - the English Space Agency's carefully orchestrated, top-secret plan that had almost actually resulted in Alara's death even though its intention was to only *make* the people of Earth think she was close to dying had been a success. People were once more interested in their work, and with such interest came innumerable donations and sponsors. Alara had single-handedly secured the financial stability of her one-way trip to Mars.

Hu-man

"Hu-man?" the alien asked in its stunted form of English. I guess people had just thought her Polish, or something. It certainly sounded Eastern European. But I knew differently.

"Yes," I confirmed. "You? Are you Martian? Or Venusian? Or…?"

"None. I am… none. I am hu-man."

I laughed. I couldn't stop myself. "No, you're not. You're really not."

"Why? Why am I… not hu-man?"

"For starters, you have horns sprouting from your head. You have pointing ears, and you have three eyes. How did nobody notice those before?" And then it hit me. "You're a shapeshifter?"

"I…" the alien began to shake its head, but I cut it off in a heartbeat.

"A shapeshifter. That explains things. But why are you here? And why is your form wavering now?"

"You know lots… little boy. You know lots for a hu-man."

"I'm not a little boy." I laughed with scorn in my voice and the alien looked abashed. I never thought I'd be able to make an alien look embarrassed. But then, I never thought I'd be speaking to an alien.

"But - how?"

"How what?"

"How did you… work… it out? How did you… know?"

"Like I said - you don't *look* human. You've been here - how long? Have you ever seen a human with horns or three eyes or… *wings!*" I breathed the final word in amazement, for insectile wings sprouted from the alien's back before my very eyes. They fluttered daintily in the still air, creating a cumbersome layer of mist. Horripilation spread across my forearms. For yes, I was scared. The alien was changing right in front of me, and it seemed not to notice.

"I... no." The alien looked downcast.

"How long *have* you been here?"

"Most of my life."

"Why?"

"I was brought here."

"Brought here? From where?"

The alien looked up at the night sky. A full moon shone over them.

"The *moon...*" I breathed.

The alien didn't reply.

"But why is your race here?"

"The same reason yours is."

"We belong here. We own this planet. It's ours."

"It is ours, too."

"But... no... I..." I was confounded. "We were *born* here. We evolved here."

"As did we. We have... lived amongst humanity... for as long as humanity has prospered."

"I - *what?!*"

The alien blinked its three eyes in unison, staring steadfastly at my confusion.

"You've always been here?"

The alien nodded. "We originated... here. Most fled... there." Again, the alien glanced at the moon. "Some... are in flux."

"Always? You've *always* been here?"

The alien nodded again.

"Since the dawn of the universe? Since humans rose from apes?"

The alien nodded for the third time.

"Then that makes you human too, surely."

"I guess so."

"So why hide?"

"We know what humanity does with extraterrestrial life. We have... seen it."

"I..."

"You experiment. You dissect. You imprison. You torture. You kill. Why would we want that?"

She had a fair point, I conceded. "So why come out now?"

"I am..."

"You're hurt," I said, my eyes drifting down to the wound in its abdomen that I had hitherto missed in its state of fluidity. It was a gunshot wound through which a fountain of blood fell.

"Yes."

"And you can't keep your form?"

"No."

"And you fear that you'll be found? Experimented on? Tortured and imprisoned?"

"Yes."

"I won't do that to you. I won't. Come on. Come with me. I'll hide you. I'll help make you better, and then you can hide once more. You mean us no harm, I'm sure."

"But... why?"

"Why what?"

"Why would you help... me? Help... us?

"Because you're human too."

The Abyss

"Is there anybody out th- th- there?"

Alara Kim's voice broke despite her determination to remain stoic. Gemlike tears stung her eyes but she refused to allow them passage to her throat. Her trepidation threatened to spill out into insanity and Alara hastened to scrabble some form of composure together. She didn't want her final words to be incomprehensible.

"Hello? Is there anyone out there? This- this is Command Module Pilot Alara Kim, from the *Genesis* controlled flight to Mars. Can anybody hear me?" As she spoke of her ranking, Alara swelled with pride. Even in this, her bleakest of moments, she was proud of her accomplishments. She'd be remembered, even if it was for all of the wrong reasons. "The mission was a failure. I repeat, the mission was a failure. We touched down on Mars at roughly 04:44 UTC on Sunday, July 21, 2050, as intended. I... I took the first steps on the surface of the Red Planet at precisely 05:59."

In her mind's eye Alara saw herself timidly stepping on the alien planet. Everything had been awash in red: maroon rocks jutted intermittently across the dusty rust-coloured sand and valleys of carmine craters had been smoothed out by solidified lava. The red hues of Mars were like blood upon her eyes: they burned fiery and angrily. A never-ending stretch of nothingness painted with minimalist tones had greeted her. Red, and nothing else. It had been numbingly cold, too, vastly different to the climate she was so accustomed to in Los Angeles, and a slight breeze had bristled sand particles in the air, creating a cumbersome, hazy outlook at the new world. The thin atmosphere was oppressive, weighing down on her body and her mind. Alara had looked upon the Martian landscape through her visor and, despite the insipidness of the intermingling shades of red, she had experienced a moment of tranquility. Mars was beautiful.

Alara's breath had hitched in her throat and, taking in the sights of the red planet, she almost forgot to breath. In her mind, Alara saw herself taking a step forward, her heart beating discreetly as though it didn't want to distract her from the monumental simplicity of walking on an alien world by beating too quickly or too nosily. The simplest of acts were amplified by her fear of what was happening. Her movements were stunted, owing to the stature of her suit

Her foot tarnished the sand in a way in which it had never been disturbed before: a footprint was left behind. No other soul had walked those pebbly shores before and the footprint would be a perpetual reminder of this... until the thin atmosphere blew a sandstorm to mask the mere presence of humanity from existence. A solitary tear danced slowly across her rounded cheek.

The weight of the world and the universe had pressed down on Alara and she could no longer contain it. She broke down, losing herself completely.

"After returning to the module," Alara continued, her voice sounding faraway as she basked in the vision of herself and her former glory, "we made preparations for the descent of *Genesis Base One*. But... but... we were attacked." Her voice cracked again as emotion swept across her. She could no longer prevent the tears that began to fall, splashing on the inside of her visor like the raindrops of Earth on a windowpane. Those beautiful raindrops which she'd never see again. Her tears distorted the recorded image, but Alara continued unimpeded. "We were attacked," she repeated in a hollow voice that sounded detached from her body as though somebody else was speaking through her. Not for the first time she wondered whether the aliens that had attacked *Genesis* were the same that her brother had encountered four years previously, she shapeshifter she had discovered hidden in his basement. "I alone managed to escape. Captain Johansson jettisoned my escape pod and I watched the attack from afar. I don't know what really happened. I don't know who attacked us. I saw several spacecrafts of unknown origin open fire upon *Genesis* until... until it was destroyed."

She paused again, trying to draw together some dignity, but the emotion was too powerful. She could see the ruin of *Genesis* before her as though it was happening again. She would never forget the golden spaceships flaring blindingly beneath the sun, firing bursts of green energy that rained like diseased fire upon *Genesis,* obliterating it instantly. The golden cubes had then dispersed, failing to see Alara's escape pod hurtling towards her impending death. She knew death was imminent, though she could not help resenting her colleagues. They had died instantly, together; they had had an easy way out. Alara did not. Sitting right above Mars, Alara had no hope of returning home. She would have to wait an unfathomable amount of time until the sun cooked her in the pod like a Sunday roast, or the food and oxygen ran scarce, or the gravity stabilisation failed. Many and more outlandish deaths awaited her. She suspected that she had always known such a prospect would befall her: the colonising mission to Mars had been a one-way expedition.

But she didn't want to die alone.

"It's now 17.48 UTC on Saturday, August 17, 2050. I've survived in this pod for almost a month. I don't know how long I have left. I don't even know if anybody is listening. I *do* know I will never return to Earth. I'll die here." As she spoke, Alara looked around the escape pod. The metal bars holding the panes of shield screen had become mullions signalling her inescapable imprisonment and her railed bed had become her coffin. Innumerable lights blinked from computer terminals around the circular room, mesmerising her as they oscillated from red to green and back again. The escape pod would be her final resting place. Her voice broke as she continued: "I don't want to die alone. I don't- If my family is there, tell them that I love them. That I miss them. That I- Starla. I'm sorry. I should never have left you. Remember me. Remember your mother and be proud. Whenever you look up at the night sky, search for the brightest star and that'll be me, Starla, looking down on you. D- d- don't forget me."

Wrought in emotion, Alara lurched forward and turned off the monitor. Intermittently throughout her month-long incarceration she had fruitlessly attempted to patch through to her family back on Earth, for monthly video-calls home had been one of the conditions of her signing up for the lifelong mission. But the calls had failed to connect and the bleeping of the dialling tone had grown more and more maddening until her attempts became increasingly interspersed. Seeking solace from something else, she rushed to the windowpanes and peered out at the planet below. Nothing remained of *Genesis* but dust and debris blinking benignly beneath a bleeding sun, half-eclipsed by the Red Planet. The bodies had long-since disintegrated. But it wasn't *Genesis* she sought.

Despite her predicament Alara still found cosmic beauty in the red orb that hung heavily beneath her and she drank in its bask. She had grown up seeing images of Mars beamed back to Earth but those images didn't give justice to the immensity of its aesthetic up close. Everything about it was red. Its tan surface emanated an inviting warmness and its auroral splay of natural lights enraptured Alara. Depending on Alara's mood, the reds of Mars occasionally looked dull and faded. Sometimes they flared as dark as blood or as black as the abyss. Sometimes she liked to imagine that the very planet was alive, and that its many shades of red were flicking flames of a powerful fire, spreading warmth and a burning desire to continue living, banishing the darkness of the eternal abyss of space. Mars had always had an intoxicating hold over her, a hold that had strengthened as she had grown. Its powerful mystique had brought her here, to this very moment, and now that she was here it maintained her possessively. She could not look away. She stared hungrily at the planet, wishing she were on it. She had become the first human to step upon the Red Planet; she longed to be the first human to die there, too.

With nothing else to do but gaze at Mars, Alara stared and stared.

Time moved on.

Alara had long since given up hope of returning home. She knew that Mars could be witnessed with the naked eye from Earth and yet she had failed to locate Earth in the expanse of inky black space. Instead she had seen a conglomerate of clustered comets streaking ceaselessly across her field of view, spreading comae and flaring in novas to momentarily eclipse everything before her. She had seen aerolites battling with asteroids across an annular nebulous of diffused reds and stark blues. She had seen innumerable stars scintillating as they orbited the photosphere of the distant sun and she had been battered by harsh solar winds that had threatened to upturn the escape pod as they scratched at the shield screens. She had seen countless beauties in the abyss of space and yet she couldn't see her home. What she could see was a quasar, a distant spot in the expanse of nothingness and she imagined this was Earth; it was this to which she looked when the reds of Mars threatened to burn her irises with their fervid flames of fulvous flares.

At the turn of the month the monotony of her autonomy furthered her growing lunacy. She ate sparingly, consuming protein packs and recycling her urine for water, grimacing as she drank. But these simplest of actions began to take their toll on her. They reminded her of Starla. She would be confidently eating solids now, something that she'd have learnt from her father. *It should have been me that taught her,* Alara thought deploringly as she chewed on her tasteless meal.

Alara thought it strange that she missed Starla so much, having nearly aborted her as a foetus. She had never wanted children. She had never wanted Starla. Her dream was to flow through the stars, and Starla's birth had set her back two years, making her the oldest member of her crew. And yet Alara had found it near impossible to bid her child goodbye after growing to love her more than she ever thought possible: a love that burned as fiery as the pulsating sun sitting at the centre of the solar system, just as Starla now sat at the centre of Alara's entire universe. *I wish I could return to her,* Alara thought as sparse tears fell from brittle eyes. *I wish I could see her, just one last time.* That was what she held out for; that was what she kept living for. And that was why she maintained her attempts at contacting her family.

She looked to the moons of Mars, Phobos and Deimos, as the beeping of her failed call grew more incessant. The misshapen satellites enriched her madness. Clawing catlike at the screen, Alara traced their deformed shapes on the pane as though each fresh attempt would yield a perfectly rounded sphere, for the unevenness of their terrains unhinged her. She saw in these tracings a reflection of her own trajectory. Her journey had been uneven with a rocky progression, just like the surface of the moons. They were pockmarked with craters, signifying the holes in her memory. As time passed she came to believe that if she could smooth out these imperfections, everything would be alright.

Hours rolled into days as she stared hungrily at the moons. The bleeping continued.

Wishing to die with somebody beside her side, Alara began to give up on her reality and feasted instead upon visions and memories of halcyon days, forgetting to live. Nightmarish spectres plagued her every moment. Her subconscious conjured images of her father's lacerated remains from his car crash and she saw herself hugging her own daughter goodbye. But Alara was destined to take the interstellar flight. Her own father had died to make it possible: despite being mesmerised by the zenith above her Alara has only been pushed to apply for the English Space Agency after hearing about her father's mission to the moon, continuing his legacy. Her father had never seen Alara grow up. *I'll never see Starla grow up,* Alara realised sickeningly and blindly sought the computer terminal again. The shrill beep permeated the silence of space.

Alara held frail hopes.

These unreachable chimeras quickened Alara's descent into insanity. She had known madness once before when Starla had been born and she had fallen so far into the abyss that she believed she'd never be able to escape. The abyss had claimed her once more for itself now, only this time its pull was much more powerful. For in the abyss Alara saw visions of Starla. Her desire to reunite with the daughter she had never really wanted maintained the abyss' grasp upon her and Alara all too willingly allowed its hold.

Anything to keep the visions coming.

Anything to see Starla.

Alara did not regret her journey through the stars for she had achieved everything she had wanted since being a little girl, peering wondrously up at the night sky. She had become the first person to stand on an alien planet. But as the abyss darkened her outlook on everything, what was once beautiful became grotesque. The flickering flames of Mars' shades of red faded to unsightly dying embers, and its malformed moons became more oblate. She no longer bothered with recycling and cleaning her urine and ate only when the pangs of hunger became too much and she lost her concentration on Phobos and Deimos. They became the only specks of light in an inky blue stretch and Alara saw nothing else. She no longer saw the distant quasar and nor did she search for her home. Instead she imagined that she was Phobos and Starla was Deimos, both circling one another in a never-ending dance, coming close but never reuniting. The yearn to be with Starla ate away at her mind as dehydration and malnourishment ate away at her body. She found that the longer she looked the less strength she had to move or trace the moons upon the panes of glass, and so she simply sat and traced them with her dried, unblinking eyes.

It was as though the moons were playing with one another, and as Alara's grasp upon her sanity slipped further away her sense of space became heightened; she imagined the moons were circling one another much faster than was possible. At their periastron

Alara felt her own heartbeat slow as she desperately willed them to collide with one another, to meet and become one. *Perhaps if they crash it'll smooth out the imperfections,* she thought as her wasted eyelids closed over parched eyes, sticking slightly due to an absence of moisture. *Perhaps if they crash, the force of the explosion will blast me back home.*

But Alara knew such hopes were futile and so she continued to call home.

The days rolled on.

Alara began to see what she wanted to see and not what was really happening, as though her mind and her vision were no longer in synchronicity with one another. Phobos and Deimos became rounder as she stared at them. The deep craters of basalt rock dotted across the surface of the asteroids hid many things, she knew. *The more I stare, the more I'll discover,* Alara thought, though she needed no encouragement in her observations. She no longer saw Deimos as Starla; rather she came to believe that Starla was hidden on the dark side of the moon and it was for this reason that her calls weren't answered. Deimos patrolled the abyss as the prison warden, maintaining the distance between mother and daughter, blocking the calls.

But Alara knew that Starla was close because she could hear her laughing. The laugh was high and shrill, with a harsher edge as it reached its terrible crescendo. It was like a cat mewling, so sharp it could cut through the shield screen, so melancholy it could induce tears even from Alara's unyielding eyes. It was the laugh of somebody in pain. A tortured laugh. It echoed with the constant beeping of the failed connection.

"Hello?"

The laughter ceased.

A voice spoke through Alara's trancelike state, an impossible voice that sounded faintly familiar. A child's voice. She looked around wildly, finally snapping her eyes off of the entrancing moons.

"Hello?"

The voice came again, not unalike Alara's own. It was timid and uncertain.

Alara's arid eyes fell on the computer terminal with its oscillating lights and its screen flaring with static. Heart hitched, Alara scrabbled forward, reaching desperately for the microphone.

"H- Hello? Is there anyone there?"

"Hello?" the childlike voice asked again.

"This is Command Module Pilot Alara Kim, from the *Genesis* controlled flight to Mars," Alara said, the words slipping off of her dried and unused tongue; she had said them so often. "Who is this?"

"Star—"

A burst of static broke through the connection, interrupting the call and the flow of speech. But Alara had heard enough. *Star.* Her heart began to thump harder than it had for nearly two months and she spoke with an urgency.

"Please repeat."

"Starla."

Tears welled in Alara's broken eyes instantly. They fell, thick and fast, hydrating her cracked skin. Gasping for air, Alara struggled to speak as the immensity of the situation fell over her. *Finally, after all these weeks, after all this time…* "Star- Starla? Is that really you?"

"Yes, it's me, mummy."

Mummy. The tears continued, relentlessly falling from aching eyes. Alara had barely dared to believe that she would speak to her daughter again and, now that she was, she had no idea what to say. She could speak no words of comfort; Starla's mother would not be returning. But she spoke anyway, of anything and nothing, drinking in the sound of Starla's voice that enriched her with a renewed sense of purpose. This was what she had continued to live for.

"Are… are you oh- okay?"

"Yes. I miss you, mummy."

"I miss you too, baby. I miss you so"—static burst across the connection and the pixilations on the screen gave way to an image hidden beneath them. Alara could see the outline of her daughter, but the snowdrop dots continued to swirl—"much. I miss you."

"Mummy—" static burst again, echoing loudly through the pod. Alara had no idea how much time they had left. She stared, unblinkingly, at the screen, willing the pixilations to collate into an image. She just wanted to see her daughter one final time; everything would be worth it for that instance. "—you?"

"What?"

"Where are you—"

"I don't know, baby girl, I don't know."

"Are you in the sky, mummy?"

"Yes! Yes…"

"Can you see me mummy?"

No, Alara thought, as she looked to the noise flaring across the screen. She closed her eyes and pictured her daughter instead. The image struggled to form within her mind. It had been so long. "Yes," she said, lying to her daughter to give her some form of comfort, some form of closure. "Yes, baby." Static flared once more and Alara peeled open her eyes to look to the screen. The pixilations were slowly forming an image, but the connection continued to waver. She didn't know if it would hold. "Yes, I see you."

"I don't see you," Starla replied, her voice so alike her mother's. Broken and emotional.

"Where are you?" she asked her daughter.

"I don't know. There's a rocket."

"Do you see the rocket?" Alara asked, knowing instantly where her daughter was; it was the only place in which the connection would be able to reach. The English Space Agency.

"Yes."

"Is it dark, baby?"

"Yes."

"Look at the sky." Alara paused as static burst once more. She didn't want her speech to be interrupted. "Are you looking? Starla, are you looking?"

"Yes."

"What do you see? Tell me what you see."

"I don't know, mummy."

"What do you see? Tell me!"

"The… the moon, mummy. I see the moon. The full moon."

"And?"

"Stars."

"Yes. How many are there? Count them for me."

"Okay. Okay. One… two… three… there's lots, mummy. Lots and lots."

"Find the brightest one, baby," Alara said as she began to fiddle with the countless wires sprouting like roots from the computer, hoping that one of them would give life to the picture. Her desperation was unhinging her, when she so desperately wanted to cling onto her flailing sanity. "Do you see it?"

"I think so, mummy."

"That's me, Starla. That's me."

"I don't- I don't understand…"

"That's me, looking down on you. Whenever you feel lonely, or you miss me, or you need— you need your mum… your mummy… look for the brightest star, Starla, and you'll see me. I'll always be there, looking for you. Looking at you. Don't forget me."

The tears soaked her dried skin, cracked and scaly. She yanked at cables, pulling them out madly, and pushing them into different connections; she flicked switches and pressed buttons and twisted knobs; she smacked the side of the computer. The screen went black.

"I see you mummy," her daughter said through the darkness of the abyss. "I see you. Mummy, do you see me? Mummy?"

A burst of static illuminated the screen and Alara momentarily became transfixed. The image was faint, cracked with static and flickering, but Alara saw Starla for the first time in three years. Her daughter had inherited her dark hair, which flowed well past her shoulders, and her wide eyes were leaking tears, mimicking Alara's own. She stared into them as the cackle-like laughter began again.

"Mummy? Do you see me?"

"Yes... Yes, baby girl. I see you!"

The image faded to white and then finally black and the static ceased. Silence fell, silence bar a barrier of lunatic laughter. Alara laughed so hard that she didn't even notice that the computer had never been active.

Tearing off her visor, Alara lurched to the shield screen and peered at Phobos and Deimos. Their never-ending chase was continuing; mother and daughter, prisoner and captor. Entranced, Alara willed them to unite. They were growing closer, she could tell. *Please,* she thought. *Reunite.*

From out of the abyss Starla floated.

Her baby girl hung before the pod, her hair flying away from her as though she was submerged beneath water. She opened her mouth and the laughter spewed, high and shrill and melancholy. Starla stretched out her hand, beckoning Alara. Alara stared, pressing her hands to the screen as Deimos highlighted Starla from behind. *The warden approaches,* Alara thought, aghast.

So entranced that she was, Alara didn't notice the first crack spread like lightning across the screen.

Her heart thumped her daughter's name as she stared.

Star-la. Star-la. Star-la.

It swelled as her daughter floated closer, beckoning Alara.

Star-la! Star-la! Star-la!

The laughter continued to laugh; the chasing moons continued to chase, much faster than was possible; the cracks continued to spread.

Star-la! Star-la! Star-la!

The first of the cracks deepened and burst and through it came a zephyr of compressed dead air. Instantly Alara felt her lungs dry and harden. Her skin became wind burned. Next came a flash of blinding white light, a quasar in distance, as though seen from the far end of a long tunnel, and in that moment what Alara had never believed came to fruition. A quick succession of images flared across her eyes, as though she was watching a sped-up movie about her own life. A deep release of adrenaline slowed down everything and Alara saw her life flash before her eyes: her mother holding her hand and bidding her farewell on Alara's first day of school; Luna and Selena hitting her, punching her repeatedly in the stomach; the car crashing with her father inside; the first time she held Starla; hugging Starla goodbye; the first time she put her spacesuit on.

An influx of air pulled Alara towards the light and she gladly accepted its push.

She was sucked from the pod towards Starla, and out into the abyss.

The Astronauts

The astronauts headed out into space. Their aim was to seek life. They left the relative comfort of their home planet, and headed into the endless abyss.

They had no idea what they'd encounter.

Jupiter and Mars whizzed by as their spaceships fled through the constellations. The astronauts marvelled at such beauty, but they knew these planets were barren.

They followed a signal; they knew life awaited them. Their sensors blinked green.

On and on they flew in the hunt for existence.

Finally, a planet loomed up before them: starkly blue, and marvellously fertile.

The aliens arrived on Earth.

They Were A Family

Atlas Kim laughed joyfully as he chased Hypnos through the trees at the bottom of the garden, his own little self-dubbed *den*. Though there was 5 years between them, Atlas and Hypnos were inseparable. Closer than cousins. More like siblings.

Juno Kim called to the children but they didn't hear.

"Leave them be," said Mars. He looked at the mountain of food before him: platters of burgers - beef and chicken - mounds of hotdogs and a basket of fish, accompanied by a forest of salad. "You've made so much. There'll be plenty left over."

Juno smiled. She looked once more at Atlas and Starla, visible through the bushes that encased the bottommost part of the expansive back yard, before settling into her seat. She turned to Sol.

"What would you like?"

"None of that," Sol said, dismissively waving her hand at the burgers and hotdogs. She peered at the fish.

"Cod and salmon," Juno said, answering the unasked question.

"I'll have a bit of salmon."

Mars placed it on his mother's plate with a pair of tongs; Juno heaped salad beside it. Sol bowed her head and prayed in private. She was the only one there that believed, so they allowed her a moment of silence as Mars and Juno dolled out food to the rest: Starla, Jace and Dionysus. Io and Jovian slept, swaddled in blankets, in the Moses basket beside Starla.

When Sol finished her prayer she glanced skywards. The evening was pleasantly warm; a soft breeze danced amongst the trees. The sun was slowly setting. Already Mars could see the faint silhouette of a gibbous moon appearing in its stead. Mars knew what his mother was thinking without asking. He was thinking the same. As were Starla and Jace, most likely. They were wishing that Alara was there. It had been over 13 years since she had arrived on Mars. They hadn't heard from her once since. The English Space Agency had told them that Alara and her fellow astronauts were safe and well in the hostile environment of their new home, but Mars was starting to think otherwise. She had signed up in '47 to head to the red planet and had told them that monthly calls home were one of the requirements she demanded, but the calls had long since stopped.

Something happened to her up there, Mars thought as he assembled his burger. Seeded bun, a heap of salad, lashings of sauce. *Probably happened to 'em all. And the Space Agency refuse to tell us. What else have they lied about?*

Laughter from the bottom of the garden brought him from his reverie. Atlas and Hypnos were both overcome with fits of giggles. Hypnos' laughter was hypnotic, and Mars found himself smiling. Alara *was* there with them, in spirit and in heart. She was his blood, and Hypnos' and most of the rest, too. They were a family. All of them.

They ate. They spoke of the past and the future, of Io and Jovian growing up, of Hypnos and Atlas moving into their next year at school. They didn't speak of Alara or their father. They didn't need to.

"Leave the dishes," Mars' mother said when they were all finished. Atlas and Hypnos still played at the bottom of the garden. The sun had dropped considerably. Darkness was starting to creep across the grass. Juno would insist they came soon. She didn't like them playing that far down when it was dark. "I'll help you with them in the morning." She proffered a rare smile then. Sol Kim smiled so rarely. Mars always had the impression that his mother was hiding something from him, a long-held secret that ate away at her insides, but in reality he suspected her refusal to express love and admiration for those around her arose from the death of her husband and the departure of her daughter.

She's scared she's going to lose us all, Mars thought.

Juno returned the smile. "Don't be daft, it won't take long. And anyway, Mars will help."

"Will I?" Mars flashed a playful smile, before beginning to gather the plates.

"Starla, come get another bottle of wine," Juno said. "And once the dishes are done, I'll call Atlas and Hypnos up." Juno glanced warily at Atlas' den. Both children were still visible, just, but it wouldn't take long until the darkness swallowed them entirely.

Starla kissed Io on the forehead as she stood. Io stirred, lids fluttering, before closing in a sleep-filled haze. She followed Mars and Juno into the kitchen.

"This has been fun," Starla said.

Mars deposited his plates on the counter and began to run the tap. Though they had a dishwasher, Juno still preferred to wash by hand, and Mars was tired of the underhand remarks she threw his way whenever he powered up the dishwasher. It was as though she didn't trust it. He conceded he could understand why.

"We need to do it more often," Juno agreed, heading out to gather the rest of the plates.

Mars began to wash the dishes. "There are a few more bottles in the fridge," he said over his shoulder, before adding: "Don't you dare try and help. Have a drink."

"Okay." Mars could hear the smile in Starla's voice as she opened the fridge and selected another bottle. "See you in a few."

"Best leave some for me."

"Can't promise anything."

And with a chuckle, she was gone.

Juno came in with the remaining dirty dishes and placed them with the rest. "I take it I'm drying?"

"Yep," Mars said, and that was that. He smiled as Juno leant in and kissed him.

Juno dried a plate with a cloth before putting it in the cupboard. She reached for a knife.

"Fu— Ahhhh!"

"Shit, are you alright?" Mars threw the sponge in the dish and grabbed a clean towel, drying his hands quickly. He moved to Juno. Blood dripped from her finger. It was a shallow cut. Tiny, really. But it was enough.

In quick succession horns sprouted from Juno's head, her ears sharpened and a third eye burst from her forehead. Insectile wings warped from between her shoulder blades.

"*God.*"

Mars quickly looked through the open kitchen door. The others were still gathered around the table, Starla pouring wine into their empty glasses. He held the towel over Juno's finger - which had turned bright blue and was beginning to arch into a claw - and squeezed firmly, hoping to staunch the flow of blood. The pressure worked, and her alien visage faded almost as quickly as it had come.

Juno looked up at him and smiled shyly. Still holding onto her finger, Mars leant over, opened a nearby drawer, and grabbed a box of bandages. Awkwardly, one-handed, he removed the packaging, biting it off with his teeth, before wrapping it around Juno's finger. Her alien appearance returned when he removed the blood-soaked towel; her humanity fluttered back from the pressure of the bandage.

"Thanks," Juno muttered, looking down at her finger. Avoiding his gaze. "I don't like you seeing me like that. I reminds me of…"

"I know." Mars was thinking it too. It reminded her of when she had been found in his shed, shortly after he had first met her. She was still in her alien guise, for her gunshot wound hadn't fully healed. The hunter had somehow traced her to the shed and was ready to strike the killer blow. But Juno had managed to get in first.

They had buried his body together.

Juno wasn't really *Juno*. Mars had married Juno at the age of 21. She had died, aged 29, birthing Atlas. Overcome with grief, Mars had asked the alien - his secret friend, whom he had protected and helped recuperate - to take on her form, so that he didn't have to explain to his son about his mother's death. He didn't want his son to feel guilty, knowing he would probably blame himself once he grew up and understood that she had died in childbirth.

And, in time, they had come to love one another. It wasn't the same, not quite, but it was close. They were a family, or as close as they could be.

From outside a scream rent the air. Followed by a cacophony of confused cries and chatter.

They saw her, Mars thought and, looking at Juno, he could tell she was thinking the same. Tentatively, scared, hand-in-hand, they walked outside.

Atlas and Hypnos were running from the bottom of the garden to the table; Sol and Starla clawed at them as they arrived, pulling them in close. Protectively.

Jace stood, face skyward. Mars followed his gaze.

Up above lights streamed across the darkened sky. They seemed to move in sequence, pulsing as they descended from the atmosphere. Around him, in nearby gardens and from windows and doors, Mars heard the confused and scared mutterings of his neighbours and friends. And then the lights came into focus.

He

He danced and he dated and he died.

That was his life from beginning to end. He sucked milk from his mother's nipple, juice from his beaker cup, lager from his pint glass, whiskey from his tumbler, and fluids from his IV drip. His first breath gave him life; his final haggard intake robbed him of his humanity.

But between those bookending moments he lived. Always striving for more, he had no regrets when his time finally came. He'd danced whenever he could, dated whomever he met. Such was the same with his death. It came swiftly and he embraced it.

The Lightning-Struck Cubes, or: The Kinds

The aliens came at the turn of the season.

The remarkable thing about their arrival was that it, coincidentally, timed perfectly with the fatal heart attack that sent Jupiter Kim crashing to the floor. He cracked his head on the corner of an end table on his way down. He was 81 years old; his reflexes were shot. He didn't have the time or the strength to thrust a hand out to try and prevent the head injury.

The remarkable thing about Jupiter's death was that, estranged as he was, it occurred at roughly the same time that the rest of the Kim family were stood, in unison, in Mars and Juno's back yard. They were a family. And Jupiter was no more.

*

The aliens came in perfect cuboids, roughly the size of an average house. No one could explain the crash of thunder that rumbled across the sky as they descended, nor the forks of lightning that crackled across the sky to crack it in two. Blue-yellow arcs frazzled off of one of the cubes and ricocheted across the rest. They continued their descent unimpeded.

*

They dubbed it The Third Kind.

Note:

The first kind: visual sightings of an unidentified flying object.

The second kind: UFO event in which a physical effect is felt, such as the malfunctioning of technology or a physiological effect on a witness (paralysis, heat, discomfort etc.)

The third kind: UFO encounters in which an animated creature is present, including robots or a human that appears to pilot said UFO.

The fourth kind: UFO event resulting in the abduction of a human.

The fifth kind: UFO event that involves direct communication between aliens and humans.

The sixth kind: the death of a human or animal as a result of a UFO sighting.

And, the seventh kind: the creation of a human/alien hybrid, either by sexual reproduction or by artificial means.

Though you could probably argue it encompassed the first, second, fifth and sixth kinds, too.

*

The aliens resembled humanity's quintessential archetype of an alien: bulbous green heads housed brains the size of basketballs; wide, distended eyes layered in two lids opened diagonally and vertically, with nicitating membranes maintaining moisture; and narrow, sticklike arms and legs held up slim bodies that looked incapable of supporting their gigantic craniums.

Humanity expected them to come, gun-blazing, ready to probe and enslave them all.

But instead they brought peace and tranquillity, medicine and technology. In hindsight, they were giving humanity a year of heaven before unleashing hell. No one quite understood why.

*

They called themselves *the Zephyr.*

Note:

Zephyr.

/'zɛfə/

Noun

1. Literary: a soft gentle breeze.

2. Historical: a fine cotton gingham.

*

Thousands of green men marched through the streets, arms laden with answers to the problems faced by humanity. They told humanity how to grow food underwater and on barren landscapes.

They told humanity how to harness the power of the sun and claim its energy as their own. They told humanity how to extend life, and how to prevent and cure numerous diseases. By the turn of the next season they had humanity enraptured. They became deities. Earth became united. Religious schisms ceased.

Africa was evacuated. The exodus of its populous spread the Africans across the world and the continent became a Brobdingnagian farm that fed the world and ended poverty. The Zephyr landed their cubes in the middle of the Atlantic Ocean to form a gigantic landmass. This became their continent, bobbing like apples in a barrel.

As the next season came the Zephyr questioned the old religions. They questioned humanity's old faith and they questioned humanity's old gods. They asked why humanity believed in what they couldn't see. This planted a seed of doubt. The newly-united world grew disdainful with the Zephyr's probing, claiming that the aliens were poised to rob them of their history. And questions were asked. Were the aliens playing a long game by tricking humanity into worshipping them so that their invasion went more smoothly? So that they became the religion of Earth? This seed of doubt, when watered, grew into a forest of uncertainty.

*

The first sign of something amiss came 10 months after their arrival.

Starla Kim headed to the corner shop to buy a copy of her friend, Sebastian's, newspaper. She bought milk, too, fancying a coffee.

Later, she sat, coffee in hand, and opened the newspaper. It was empty.

Words

'If all Printers were determin'd not to print any thing till they were sure it would offend no body, there would be very little printed.'

- Benjamin Franklin, 10 June 1731

There are no journalists. There are no authors. There are no writers.

Only **words**.

"Oscar Wilde will be turning in his grave," Starla Kim said, her blue eyes fixed squarely on the shelf before her. Her pigtail hairstyle suggested immaturity, but a nubile head sat on youthful shoulders. "Joseph Conrad will be turning in his grave. William Shakespeare will be turning in his grave." She began to list them all: Virginia Woolf, Thomas More, Robert Louis Stevenson, Jane Austen, Mary Shelly, Stephen King. All had written controversial tomes. None would be published again.

The shelf before her was empty.

Blankets of dust revealed where the books had previously stood, though all had long since been burned.

"Such is the way," responded Sebastian Croft, a stressful young man who was recently out of work. His tousled hair was prematurely balding, painting him older than his years.

"How can Oscar Wilde cause offence?" Starla deplored.

"You *did* read the book, right?"

"Of course I did."

"It's quite easy to understand how his work could offend some," conceded Sebastian. "And the printers—"

"Refuse to work, I know. But *why*?"

"I don't know. I wish that I did. I've tried every conceivable measure, and they still refuse to impart words. Everything offends someone."

"Show me. Show me your press."

They journeyed through a bland London town void of advertisements, billboards, and signs. A pub once known as 'The Horses Trough' now caused offence to vegans and farmers alike, and its sign had been torn down. Automated electronic billboards advertising cars and movies had had their words stripped away, leaving only an image behind, and Starla suspected it was only a matter of time before printers refused to print images. Images could be just as offensive as words, she knew.

They arrived at Sebastian's office, where Sebastian took his usual stance before the printing press, willing the cogs to work. It was an old model, and Starla thought that perhaps this was why it was no longer working. But it hadn't printed a thing in days, and its inkwells were slowly running dry. Sebastian heaved a sign of despair and lifted a hand to run through his hair, before replacing it swiftly at his side, fearing that touching his hair would draw more strands from their roots. He fidgeted absentmindedly with the zipper of his jacket, despairing at the world.

The printing press was coated in a thin shield of dust that protected it from use. But even that was offensive. Sebastian found it offensive. The press should be whirring and groaning, churning out coagulated ink into beautiful strings of words and photographic reminders of the wondrous world around them. But there it sat, stationary, mockingly so.

"This is the last thing it printed," Sebastian said, handing Starla a sheaf of paper from his desk behind them. The paper branded an article on The Arrival with sparse words, reading as such:

Yesterday (September 11th), the Prime Minister said and that   before leaving the party.   stated that a bill to tackle   was in place, and that fellow MPs would be able to vote for or against the matter.

The bill proposes that those who   should seek asylum   . The home Secretary agreed with   claims by adding that   .

Starla could not read on.

The printing press refused to impart offensive words lest others became offended, and apparently the term 'alien' and 'extraterrestrial' could cause offence. Once more Sebastian raised his hand to his hair, before timidly scratching at his beard instead. The press simply would not print a thing that could cause offence. It refused to print the term 'rainbow', lest homosexuals took offence, and nor would it print the pronouns 'he' or 'she', in case this caused offence to either sex, or those that identified as neither. It would not print out colours, countries, names. In fact, it barely printed much at all. Printing only half a story was no story at all, and Sebastian had conceded that he could no longer run his newspaper.

He argued that anything could cause offence if people so wished to interpret the written word as such, and that it was simply a matter of individuality, but the press would not listen. Frustrated, Sebastian kicked the press, receiving nothing more than a throbbing foot.

"Have you tried—" began Starla.

"Probably," cut in Sebastian.

"What about—"

"Most likely."

"Or—"

"Yes. I've tried everything."

"Oh." Now it was Starla's turn to slump in defeat.

"And it's not just the printers," said Sebastian. He looked over at Starla. "Do you ever get the feeling that you can't say what you really mean?"

"What I really mean?" Starla repeated, confused. "Whatever do *you* mean?"

"I think things, sometimes, and I even go as far as saying them aloud, but... it's like the words refuse to come. Like I've forgotten them, or something. Like I've forgotten how to speak. It's only certain words, certain phrases," he said dismissively.

"What words?"

Sebastian swallowed hard. He wished he hadn't said anything now.

"The words that the printers refuse to print. It started much in the same way that the printers did. The printers initially stopped printing words that *I'd* find offence in." He blushed a little, but continued. Or rather, he *tried* to continue, but the words wouldn't leave his mouth. He swallowed hard. "They won't come," he said. "The words won't come."

"Can you write them down?" suggested Starla.

"I'll try."

Sebastian pulled a sheaf of paper to him and scribbled down the three words. He passed the paper to Starla. She read them, all three of them: Bald. Boring. Literate.

She looked up.

"Try and say them aloud," said Sebastian.

So she did. She thought the words, she opened her mouth, but they wouldn't come out.

"I don't... I don't understand," she said.

"Go outside. Go outside and try again."

So she did. The words came out with swift ease. Perplexed, she rushed back up to tell Sebastian.

"You can't say them in front of me," he said. "And I bet the same goes for me. Go on, write down some words that you find offensive."

So she did. Sebastian read them, and tried to read them aloud, but the words would not come. He exited his office, and the words came easily. "Female. Failure. Child."

He re-entered the office with a grim look on his face. "It's only going to get worse, I fear."

And it did. Slowly, more and more people began to notice that they could no longer speak certain words in front of certain individuals. At the same time the printing presses stopped printing photos. Of anything. They stopped printing all together. Then pens and pencils stopped working, as did keyboards and mobile phones. The written word became defunct. Memos were delivered blank, unaddressed envelopes were pushed through letterboxes at random, and film production ceased. Slowly, the spoken word became defunct too.

Earth, turning majestically, soaked in rays of sunlight to feed the populous below. But the planet was silent, bland, uniform. Nobody spoke. Nobody wrote. No machinery croaked. No animals bleated. A blanket of banality adopted the planet.

There are no journalists. There are no authors. There are no writers.
There are no...

A Facade

Raindrops mask my tears. Though I'm swamped amongst the dead I'm alone. I feel alone. I don't remember what it's like to feel differently. That time has gone. Now? Now I must conform to expectations. I must appear as though I'm carrying on. If only for Starla's sake. She manages. Too much time has passed; surely I should be over it? But no. I'm not.

I wish I could climb inside the grave just for once final embrace with my son. I wish I could say a proper goodbye. I wish... I wish so much.

I go home. I look at photos. I swallow the pills.

Utopia / Dystopia / Utopia?

Atlas Kim read of utopian ideals by Thomas More when his world ended.

It was rather out of the blue: one moment he was engrossed in the description of Amaurot; the next his idealist land descended into a dystopia. It was almost as though the book was condemning the society from which he belonged, just as More had condemned his own society five-hundred-years previously.

Fire raged all around, burning everything in sight, and a heavy layer of ash threatened to suffocate him. His family was torn apart. The city lay in ruins, with half-buried buildings slumbering in shadows of yesterday. Hell had consumed them all.

From out of his ruinous familial abode Atlas scrambled. Nothing remained. Nothing bar the book he had been so infatuated with. Dystopia had arisen, but a new utopia now had a chance of thriving.

Torn

Dust and debris decimated the district. The third kind had left Earth a ruin.

The howling of the wind cut like the jagged fork of the aliens' laser beam, eliciting memories of murderous pasts, and Starla Kim shivered. Everything before her was in ruin: buildings lay half collapsed like slumbering giants; smouldering tree trunks stood like grotesque memories of what they once were; the riverbed was barren and arid; and the streets were littered in the remnants of humanity. Cracked bones lay all around. The street had been painted red with spilled blood, some of which still bubbled and popped.

Starla tentatively stepped forward. She didn't want to stand on the bones of her former friends and neighbours.

"What are you looking for?"

At first the question evaded her. Perhaps her words were blanketed in the screeching wind; perhaps Starla chose to ignore them. She wasn't entirely sure what she sought. But she asked her again and again, and Starla eventually repented.

"Her." The word were terse and choked. Despite herself, Starla cried. She looked upon the osseous remains around her with covetous eyes, wishing desperately that she could join them. She had survived when so many others had perished. It was unfair and unjust.

"Starla, why? You know she isn't here."

"I don't know that," was Starla's response. She looked all around, her hair billowing in her wake. She looked strangely ethereal, strangely demonic.

"Starla - she wasn't here. She wasn't here when they came. See sense."

"Then where is she?" Starla demanded, whipping around to stare at Dionysus.

"I don't know. I don't know, but she isn't here."

"They ruined everything," Starla whispered, her voice suddenly quiet and faraway.

"What?"

"They ruined everything!"

Emotion burst from her like a fiery eruption. Her streaming tears were burning rivulets of lava, her eyes alight with fury. She whipped back round and set off again, no longer caring about stepping on bones. They crunched beneath her footfalls.

"Starla. Starla! Stop."

"I have no one left."

"You do. You have me."

"I don't. I have no one"

"Nobody does now. Everybody is gone, but we aren't. *We* have to continue."

"How?" Starla stopped again. "How do we continue, after this?"

"We just do." Dionysus took Starla's hand in her own, while tenderly stroking her other hand down Starla's face. She brushed aside her tears. "We have to, because what's the alternative?"

"What was the point?" Starla asked.

"In what? Continuing? In not giving up?"

"No, no, in them. In them coming. They came. They conquered. They left. They returned. Why? What did they achieve? What was the point in it all?"

"I don't know." Dionysus suddenly enveloped Starla in a tight embrace, and despite herself the tears fell, thick and fast. Her frail body shook beneath the weight of everything she was holding onto. "She isn't here, Starla. Surely you know that?"

"Yes." Her voice was thick. "Yes, I know. But then, where is she?"

"I don't know. We'll find her, though. There are so few of us left now - she'll turn up."

"I can't lose both my children," Starla said. "I can't." A pause. Then: "I wish my Mum was here. She'd know what to do." She felt suddenly childlike and immature.

"Do you blame her?" Dionysus asked, as Starla cast her gaze skywards. Darkness blanketed the desolation around her. The moon up above was full, grey, and bland in comparison to the red tinge that encapsulated the night sky, a tinge caused by the atmosphere of Earth slowly burning away. Stars speckled the sky, and Starla sought the largest. It was this quasar that she imagined was Mars, the red planet that had captured her mother.

"No," she said finally.

"Most do," Dionysus said. She was scared of her reaction, but felt that it needed saying regardless. "They say," she continued, "that the aliens only came because she went up there. Because *they* went up there. The Space Agency sent humans up looking for aliens, so aliens came and killed us all."

"She didn't send them personally," Starla argued. "It was a coincidence. That's all."

"And now we're to follow in their footsteps. That'll surely only enrage them further."

"Do you believe that? Do you believe that the aliens came because we went to them first? Do you think my mother killed us all?"

"I... no. I don't know. It's not your mother's fault. It's not anyone's fault, really. But they came *after* the Space Agency sent *Genesis* to colonise Mars. Surely the coincidence is too great to ignore?"

"What's done is done," Starla said simply. "We can't change anything. But I must find Io before we leave."

"She'll already be there, waiting for us. Just you watch."

"I can't go there without looking first. I'm sorry - I can't. You go, you go without me. It's okay."

"No."

"Di."

"No."

"Go."

"I'm not leaving you. You said yourself - we have no one left. I'm not leaving you. What if something goes wrong and you're stranded here when we leave? No. I'm not leaving you. But I'll forcibly take you if I have to. Earth is in ruin and Io is nowhere to be seen. Even if you do find her out here, she'll be gone. She'll be dead. And you can't bring her body with us; the radiation is too powerful. It'll wipe out the entire rocket, and take the rest of humanity with it. We're only here because we've taken radiation pills, but they'll wear off eventually. No, we have to go."

"But I can't."

Starla's voice broke asunder and tears streamed down her mephistophelian face. She was torn.

"I've lost everyone."

"We all have."

"My mother. My father. My son. My daughter. You."

"You haven't lost me," Dionysus said. "I'm right here."

"For now," Starla conceded. "But you'll fade, eventually."

"I'll always be here, though. I'll always be with you. I'll always be here." At that she lay a hand over Starla's chest, right over her beating heart. Its pulses seemed to quicken beneath her touch. "I'll be here."

"You won't when the rocket leaves. You'll stay here. I'll leave you. I can't do that. I can't leave any of you."

"You have to."

"Why?"

"Because the alternative is to die here, on Earth, and your mother wouldn't want that. I know she wouldn't. She wouldn't want you to die here, alone. Like she did up there. Go. Travel through the stars, follow in her footsteps. Leave this hellish place and prosper in the next."

"I... *can't.*"

"Io will be waiting at the rocket, just you wait and see. I'll come with you, I'll stay until you go. Just go. Please. You're not meant for this place. Look around - there's nothing left. Nothing. The third kind took everything out. You can't survive here. There's no vegetation, and the stores of food are depleting. The soil is barren. The streets are awash in blood. A sea of radiation burns away at everything. You have mere minutes until your radiation pill wears thin. Even if Io *is* here, you won't find her before your pill wears out. You have a choice. Stay and die in this dystopia. Or leave and thrive elsewhere."

"I... I..." Starla had hit a stalemate. She was torn in wanting to match her mother's lingering memory, and wanting to find her desolate daughter. But even if she did find her, Dionysus was right. Io would be dead and gone, along with the vast majority of humanity. "I'm still here," she said aloud, to herself. Then she realised that everything she had said thus far was to herself, and she barked out a bray of baleful laughter. Dionysus wasn't really there. She was dead, and Starla was talking to herself. "I'm still here. They're not."

"Exactly," Dionysus said, her words echoing otherworldly.

"I... I have to go. I... I don't have much time left. The - the rocket!"

She turned, with one last sweeping look at the bodies around her, and ran for the rocket. Dionysus joined her.

"You're doing the right thing," she called.

"Io - she has to be there. She *has* to be."

"She will be. She was right beside you when the lasers burned everything, and you survived. You'll find her again. You'll find our daughter."

The rocket loomed before them, a gleaming structure of metallic technology that juxtaposed with the ruinous city around it. The full moon was half-eclipsed behind it, bathing Starla in partial darkness.

"Go," Dionysus said when they arrived. "Embark and live. Find Io and survive. Do it for me. Do it for your mother. Do it for Io."

Starla looked to Dionysus through the window as the rocket gained traction and erupted into the air. Dionysus stood sentinel and watched her depart. And then she departed for the next life, leaving the dystopian ruin of Earth vacant of vegetation and organic sentience.

The Mockery

The missile flew at dawn.

An explosion of fire threw the rocket into the air, thrusting it towards the future. Mars was awaiting them. Below the osseous remains of humanity lay littering the streets like grotesque Halloween costumes - skeletal, deformed, discoloured; a mockery of what once was. The remnants of humanity moved on. A common goal of survival hung over them all.

The blues and greens of Earth warped into the blackness of the oppressive expanse of nothingness, an abyss of tranquility. Space stretched before them. And on the missile flew, never looking back.

267 days. 8 and a half months. 38 weeks. 6, 408 hours. 384, 480 minutes.

Mars loomed up before the missile, a ball of beautiful burning red. Starla watched through the window. Their salvation?

More or Less

The rocket kissed the sky in a bloom of alluring red and for the briefest of moments that was all anybody saw. The remnants of humanity bleeding blindly before fading from existence.

Io Kim looked up and wept as her planet died around her. Her fellow survivors did likewise. They wept not because the rocket and its saved inside had managed to escape and, hopefully, prosper elsewhere. No. They wept because they were left behind. Because they were ill. Because they were infected.

Some ran straight to Cumbria to chart the rocket's course; others stampeded through the shopping centres looting everything in sight. Some cried for their relatives that had escaped, and some partied raucously to celebrate the ending of the world.

Io did none of this. She simple sat and waited, waited for her mummy to return.

The streets were awash in gangrenous silhouettes that barely resembled humanity. Flaking skin, rotting bones, wild eyes. And yet somehow, miraculously, they stayed alive. But they were no longer human. They were more than human now. Or less, depending on how you looked at it.

But they managed to adapt, to evolve, to become something different entirely. To survive.

They became like animated corpses, like zombies that behaved, for the most part, civilised. They sat down together and ate meals. Regular meals, that is. They didn't eat each other. No, they ate roast dinners and pizza, cakes and fruits. And they continued to write books, to produce films, and to work their daily jobs. The ban on offensive words had been lifted. Io surmised it was due to The Third Kind vacating. The looting stopped; that which was looted was returned. The stolen goods formed part of somebody's business, after all, and that somebody had to earn a living.

So they continued to *act* human, but they no longer looked human. And nor did they think human, either. Not really. But they thought more or less like a human, and that was good enough for them.

*

On the starship blasting through the stars, those who were immune from the infection fled Earth on the hunt for a new exoplanet. They spared not a solitary thought for the billions they had left behind.

*

But plans were afoot and rockets were created. Thousands of them, to carry the infected through the stars, to chase humanity. After all, that was what the humans had done - built rockets and blasted off. And the infected thought like humans. More or less, anyway.

Child of the Rocket

2077: Ares Kim was born on March 30th to Atlas and Jarla Kim. He was a child of the rocket. Each rocket housed roughly 1,000 humans and pregnancies were strictly monitored and policed to ensure the population didn't exceed 1,100 - the exact figure that their homes could house. Someone had to die in order for someone to be born. There was a waiting list in place, and Jarla has signed up within weeks of the rocket's departure, despite Atlas initially being adamant that he didn't want to bring a child into their world of carnage. But Jarla had managed to change his mind, and Ares was conceived after the death of an elderly woman who was jettisoned into space as part of her funeral rights. Weighing 7 pound, 10 ounces, Ares was born with a crop of light blonde hair and the pinkest lips imaginable. Atlas and Jarla loved him from the moment they clapped eyes upon him and, though the circumstances were far from desirable, they swore to give him the best life. Earth was no more, but Ares was still human, and that counted for everything as far as they were concerned.

2078: Ares was just shy of one when the talks began. Though he understood nothing at the time, it was all recanted to him in the form of stories as he grew, so much that it eventually became a part of his very being. The mothership, which housed the world leaders that had survived, had detected two anomalies which, upon investigation, lead them to two conclusions. One: a wormhole had opened near Jupiter that could, potentially, take them to a hospitable world. Two: thousands of signals were originating from the direction of Earth, indicating not everyone had died like they had first suspected. But what to do? Wait for the rest to arrive, risking the collapse of the wormhole in the meanwhile? Or venture through and risk leaving the rest of humanity alone? Ares cooed and cawed as the adults around him discussed the possibilities.

_2080_: Ares' hair darkened just after his third birthday, but his eyes remained as inquisitive as ever. Reportedly, his first word was "Earth", with a slight infliction that Jarla swore was him questioning either what Earth was, or why they had left there. He became so obsessed with this word that, while his parents watched the unmanned probe dispatched from the mothership, Ares pointed to anything and everything and dubbed it _Earth_. He soon discovered a new word, though, and from the direction that people looked when they said it, Ares knew (perhaps intuitively) that the word didn't denote something they had left behind but, rather, something they were aiming for. The world leaders, though they were no longer leaders of a world, unanimously agreed to wait for the remnants of humanity. And what to do while they waited? Explore the moons of Jupiter, the distant spec that Ares soon became obsessed with.

_2081_: Ares didn't fully understand what his cousin, Hypnos, was telling him. He pulled a face and pushed his lips out in a pout that often adorned his face when he didn't get his way. And right now he wasn't getting his way. "What mean?" he asked, over and over, but no one answered his question. "Are you sure about this?" Ares heard his parents ask, and his aunt, and even when Hypnos said he was sure, they still refused to clue Ares in. "It's probably gonna be a suicide mission," mummy said. "Just like my mum," Aunty Star agreed. "Suicide?" Ares asked. He didn't understand the word. None of them defined it for him. Hypnos hugged him again and kissed his forehead and Ares hugged him back, even though he didn't understand what was truly happening. He didn't realise that this was the last time he would ever see his cousin and, in time, he came to forget him. But he didn't forget the word. Suicide must, he concluded, mean when people go and don't come back. Ever.

_2083_: Ares, as a child of the rocket, spoke a dozen languages by the time of his sixth birthday. He mixed with people from all across Earth and was a dab-hand at acquiring language. He knew English and Spanish, German and Hindi, Chinese and Arabic. He even knew a few choice words in Latin, the language of old. English had been adopted as the official language of the rockets, the mother-tongue through which rules and instructions and documentation was written, but that didn't mean that the other languages died out. Most on board had only spoken their own tongue when fleeing, but there were enough speakers of each to ensure that the languages weren't lost. And all picked up words of the mother-tongue, meaning most could communicate with each other. But only one Bulgarian family had survived the hellish end to Earth - one family, amongst a thousand ships. Bulgarian would soon fall foul of decay alongside Latin. The family needed to adapt, less they isolated themselves and Ares, though only six at the time, took it upon himself to teach them. He was intelligent and he was patient, traits that life on the rocket forced upon him. The Angelov family told Ares that their name translated as *the son of angel,* and Ares learnt a new word that fascinated him. He was growing into quite the orator.

2085: Ares came to understand more as he grew. His cousin, Hypnos, had been dispatched to Europa, a moon of Jupiter, after a signal had originated from the surface of the biggest planet in the solar system - despite no surface officially existing. They had gone to their death in the search for answers. Ares was told, through mouths that didn't belong to his family (for they refused to speak of Hypnos), that in times of old ESA - whatever that was - sent unmanned probes to scout out planets before risking the lives of astronauts. But times were hard now, though Ares knew no different. What he did know was this: the initial distress signal was the only signal that ever came from Jupiter. Some findings were sent from a couple of the astronauts that confirmed that they had successfully managed to terraform part of Europa and Jupiter, but they received no direct communication or discourse with the five astronauts that had, essentially, been sent to their death. "Do you ever think that maybe our family should stop pushing the boundaries of known space?" Ares once heard his father ask his aunt, Starla. She didn't respond, but her expression confirmed that she was in agreement. Ares later came to learn that his aunt had lost all of her children. He also decided something, at the tender age of eight. Despite his father's worries, Ares wanted to follow in the footsteps of the Kims. He was fully prepared to give his life if it meant discovering something, or exploring an uncharted world. All he knew was the rocket. He was longing to know more.

_2090_: Ares had his first kiss at the age of thirteen. They were stood in front of the sweeping view of space, an expanse of blackness. They had never heard from Hypnos, and the remnants of humanity still hadn't caught up with them. For now, they were playing the waiting game and, with the onset of puberty, came a desire to escape the banality of life on the rocket, to discover something brand-new. And what Ares discovered was this: love at first sight existed. Okay, so he hadn't _actually_ fallen in love the moment he had first looked at Atanas Angelov, because he had grown up being best friends with him. That was all, friends. But their friendship, that consisted of creating stories of the universe, chasing each other around the rocket, reading stories of old and playing video games, soon blossomed when Atanas made the admission that he _thought_ he liked boys. Ares had always known this about himself, for as long as he could recall, but had never openly mentioned it to anyone. Not that he was scared or ashamed. It was just he grew in a world in which the concept of revealing ones sexuality - coming out, he later learnt was the term - was never really an issue. Certainly not to those around him. His aunt had married another woman and Ares, with his parents, lived just along from a married couple of guys, who Atlas and Jarla often had round for food and drinks. Growing up, sexuality was… normal. Ares guessed that humanity had bigger fish to fry nowadays. Because of this he had never found the need to reveal his sexuality to his family. He knew there would come a day when he would introduce a boy to his parents, but that was exactly how he envisaged it: "Mum, dad, this is… and we're in love." Simple as that. No need to come out of the closet, no need to feel ashamed or scared of their reaction. But he could tell that

Atanas' admission was a big deal to him. Maybe it was because his family were religious, maybe it was because he was an only child, but Atanas was scared. Ares pointed out that, either way, the Angelov bloodline would die out before long anyway, and both boys laughed at that. That was when Ares revealed that he liked boys, too. And it just happened. One moment they were talking, as friends, The next they were kissing, as… something more? Ares certainly hoped so. Because, whilst he didn't discover that love at first *sight* existed, he certainly discovered that love at first kiss existed. His heart beat rapidly and, in that moment, he knew that he loved his best friend.

_2091_: Ares had dated Atanas in secret for almost a year, not because he wanted to keep it secret, but because Atanas did. Atanas, in Bulgarian, meant a person who is immortal, so Atanas' full name essentially meant immortal angel. Ares liked that. He didn't like the idea of Atanas dying - he wanted his boyfriend to live forever without pain. But Atanas felt that pain was coming for him. He had readied himself and, with the help of Ares, had arranged a dinner with both sets of parents. Atanas had told Ares that he was sick of living in secret and, one way of another, wanted his parents to know the truth. They sat down to dinner together. Each rocket contained a farm, through which food was distributed evenly and equally between the one thousand people onboard, meaning class and status were essentially eradicated. Bigger fish to fry. That's exactly what they were having: fish. Synthetic tuna, to be precise. And as they sat to eat Atanas stretched out his hand and took hold of Ares'. He looked expectantly up at his parents. Ares read the fear on his face. But the Angelov's, whom Ares had taught to speak English at the age of six, simply smiled. As did Ares' own parents.

_2092_: Ares couldn't help but grin at the news. His parents had added their names back to the waiting list as soon as Ares was born, and had had to wait almost fifteen years for the news that yes, they could have another child.

_2093_: Ares held his sister, Minerva Kim, who shared his dark hair and inquisitive eyes. She was another child of the rocket.

_2099_: Ares celebrated the turn of the century with his family. Aunt Starla looked forlorn. She was prone to angry outbursts or hiding away in solitude. Ares heard his parents discussing Starla's mum, and Ares' great-aunt, Alara. Apparently madness ran in the Kim family. Both Alara and Sol, Ares' great-grandmother, had fallen victim to depression, both likely due to the predicaments they found themselves in. Ares had quizzed his family to discover the story of his family; he created a tree to track them and chronicled their exploits. He now understood what his father had meant when he was eight: "Do you ever think that maybe our family should stop pushing the boundaries of known space?" His family consisted of astronauts (his great-grandfather, Artemis, his great-aunt, Alara, and his cousin, Hypnos) all of whom had died on their maiden voyage. He had lost some family on Earth, too, when hell was unleashed. His Aunt Starla had never found her daughter, Io. Ares thought she could be amongst the remnants that were still heading their way, but he didn't dare say this to his aunt. Starla had long since accepted her death. Accepted, but not recovered from. And now here they were, poised on the lip of the unnamed wormhole, awaiting the arrival of the remnants. Ares was beginning to doubt they would ever arrive.

_2100_: Ares heard that the wormhole was teetering on the verge of collapse and, so, the mothership conceded that they had to think about themselves, and forget the remnants. As one, the collective rockets, totalling almost one thousand, journeyed past Jupiter and stormed through the wormhole. Either they would find salvation, or they would find their deaths.

_2107_: Ares married his childhood sweetheart in the middle of the TRAPPIST system of planets. His parents were in attendance, alongside his sister and Atanas' father. Aunt Starla proffered a rare smile. As they shared their first dance, plans were discussed pertaining to the prospective exploration of the seven planets: b, c, e, f and g, that were reportedly a similar size to Earth, and d and h, which were closer in size to Mars. Ares hadn't found the courage to tell his parents that he was one of three being sent to TRAPPIST-1g.

_2110_: Ares was midway through a training mission - repairing a broken engine on the starship (which was designed to prepare him for conducting repairs in the extreme circumstances that he may find on TRAPPIST-1g) - when he heard the news of his Aunt Starla's passing. Though he wanted to abort the EVA and go immediately to console his father, Starla's sister, he knew that his training was of the utmost importance. There was one positive of her death, he later conceded as he hugged his father. Her death meant that another family could have a child. He held his parents' hands as Starla's body was dispatched into space. He watched as she floated peacefully away. "Good innings," was how Atlas described his sister's life. She was 66 when she died.

_2111_: Ares held the child of the rocket in his arms as Atanas read the document that declared they were officially parents. The baby boy was one years old; Ares was convinced the boy was conceived upon the pronunciation of Starla's death. Her death had indeed meant another could have a child: him. He had never really thought much about being a father, but looking down at the boy - at his son - Ares fell in love so powerfully that it hurt. They renamed him Priapus. "I'll be back before you know it," he whispered to his son, his face bent so low that his lips brushed Priapus' forehead. "A year, tops. And who knows - we might find you a new home." He looked up at Atanas, so that his husband knew these words were meant to be heard by him too. "I love you so much. And I'm coming back to you. Don't worry about that. Try and keep me away. I won't be another Kim - I won't be like the others. I'm coming back."

_2112_: Ares took his first steps on a world at the grand age of thirty-five. He was overcome with emotion and wept until his eyes ran dry. Beside him, Antoinette and Esmé wept, too. They were all children of the rocket. The rocket was all they had known. Right now they were doing what millions hadn't yet done in their lives: walk outside. It was a fantastic feeling and, despite their mission brief, Ares started to walk, then jog, then full-on run. His arms were thrown in the air as he galloped beneath the warming sun. His breathing echoed in his helmet. They had selected their landing site carefully and they had been right: liquid water swam in rivers across the surface of the planet. Most of TRAPPIST-1g was smothered in rocks, but a few faraway features across the horizon looked, to Ares, like they could be trees. But probably other rock-formations. But if there was water on TRAPPIST-1g (we really need a new name for this place, Ares thought), there was the possibility of life, either intelligent or that which would bring humanity sustenance. Could TRAPPIST-1g form a new home for humanity? Ares, Antionette and Esmé were in agreement: yes, they had found a potential Earth.2. It wouldn't be that easy, Ares knew, and it would take a long time to ready the planet for them - probably past Ares' lifespan - but Priapus could, one day, follow in his footsteps. This thought maintained Ares through his year-long incarceration on the planet, during which time his eyes feasted on the heavens as though he could see the rocket he called home, and his son. They spent the year searching the planet. Every months or so they would scramble back to their pod and set flight for a new section of TRAPPIST-1g, trying to scope out properties that could help them form a new home here. The air was breathable, in small doses, but Antionette reckoned they could grow accustomed to this and, if not, it wouldn't take much to terraform the world. And there was a weather pattern that was similar to how that on Earth had been described: scorching heat, blistering winds, torrential rain. But they found no form of life - no extraterrestrial fauna or flora, and certainly no sign of intelligence. If they were to live here, they would have to test whether the ground would support crops. Their last task before departing was to plant and water an entire farm of crops. They would be monitored from space.

2113: Ares cried as he hugged his husband and son. There would be time to tell the mothership their findings; for now all he wanted was his family.

2120: Ares didn't cry. He didn't feel anything. His father looked as though he could be sleeping. They wrapped him in blankets as his body was loaded onto the pod. Atlas Kim would not be sent into space like the millions before him. Ares had fought against that. He had risked his life journeying to TRAPPIST-1g; his payment would be a return journey to bury his father. This time he went alone. Atanas had wanted to come, but Ares had flat-out refused. What if something happened to them both? He refused to turn Priapus into an orphan. Ares buried his father at the sight of their first landing and he sat, for over an hour, at the graveside. He wanted to spend some time with his father.

2125: Ares' mother was buried beside his father. TRAPPIST-1g had, somehow, become a mass graveyard. Though the planet was hospitable, it was discovered that TRAPPIST-1d and TRAPPIST-1e bore surfaces and atmospheres that more closely resembled Earth. TRAPPIST-1h hadn't yet been explored, but that had been left for now. Plans were being drafted to send a group of astronauts to a terraformed area of TRAPPIST-1d to live in isolation for a year, a test to see if the world could support them. And so TRAPPIST-1g had become a graveyard; it was also the stopping point for the rockets and, in accordance with a strict schedule, people were finally allowed to venture out onto the planet's surface, to breath its air and to drink its water. Priapus was now fifteen, and after his grandmother's funeral he shared a drink of fresh water with his fathers.

2035: Ares was reading a book he had read a dozen times when Priapus came to him with two admissions. Area put his book - More's Utopia - down and looked at his husband. Priapus told them that one, he felt as though he was really a woman and two, he wanted to sign up for the isolation mission to TRAPPIST-1d. The gasses within the terraformed dome had been dispatched a few years previously, but it would be another few years before they were ripe for life. Ares told his son - his *daughter*, he corrected himself - the same thing for both admissions. "It's your life. You must do what you want to or what you need to and I love you regardless." He knew what Priapus was thinking, could read it in the look on her face. She didn't want to be *just* a child of the rocket. She, like him, wanted more than that.

2149: Ares tried his hardest but couldn't. He cried like a baby as he hugged Priapus goodbye. She hadn't yet transitioned; medical procedures, like everything else, was a waiting list, and unfortunately some operations had precedence over others. She hadn't decided on a new name yet, either, but she dressed like a woman and wore makeup. To Ares, she was beautiful. He was going to struggle not being in contact with her for a year, but he knew it would be worth it.

2151: Ares found it hard to move fast nowadays. He was seventy-four and, though he would have gratefully welcomed death to join his husband, he had fought against it, holding off because he didn't believe it. He knew she was still alive, despite the official documentations saying otherwise. TRAPPIST-1d wouldn't suffice as their new home, but the mothership had decided on TRAPPIST-1e - Earth.2. They wouldn't disclose their reasoning. The rockets set sail and Ares refused to give up. Refused.

2152: Ares thought that Priapus looked different. "It's Aphroditus, now," she said, hugging him. She didn't cry. Something had hardened her, and she refused to tell him what. She refused to talk about the mission, only to say that it had gone wrong, that the rest had been consumed. She didn't want to return to the ships and to humanity. She was beyond that, now. "That'll mean you're all alone," Ares said. "You won't be able to have your surgery, you won't be able to—" "I don't care," Aphroditus replied. "I don't care. I'm alive, and I don't mind being alone. I've always felt that way." "What are you going to do now?" Ares asked. His daughter eyed the pod behind him. "I'm a child of the rocket, dad, just like you. But now I want to be a child of the universe."

2155: Ares Kim died on September 11 whilst trekking - slowly, for he was seventy-eight - across the baron landscape of TRAPPIST-1h with his daughter, the only planet in this solar system that was yet to be explored. He, like his daughter, was a child of the universe now. Aphroditus returned him to TRAPPIST-1g and buried him beside his family. Beside the Kims.

Mimic pt. I

On a distant starship the five astronauts slept in hibernation. Their journey was a long one, but it was nearing its completion. Hypnos, Rafael, Ursula, Bapoto and Qadir were the best of the best. They had also woefully given up their lives on the hunt for knowledge. They would become iconic in their deaths.

Black was all around. Black tarred with the darkest blue. A smattering of stars twinkled dully, illuminated by the distant sun. The astronauts were so far from home that they felt no natural heat. Most had forgotten what home looked like. They had adopted another. The mothership they had left was their parental home; the starship they currently inhabited was their rented little flat; the awaiting moon would be their first house share; and, hopefully, the star it orbited would become their permanent abode. As the only life there, they would own the entire planet.

Hypnos awoke first. He looked out at the burnished moon ahead. It was frozen white, with streaks of golden land, and the most beautiful sight in the solar system.

One-by-one the astronauts awoke and they each feasted upon sights of their new home. Excitement fizzled in the air.

"What will we do first?" Ursula asked.

"We're to stick to schedules," Bapoto said sternly. "Build the temporary habitat, scope out the moon, and then send the probes to explore Jupiter."

"But we're gonna deviate a little, right?"

Bopoto switched off the signal that radioed their communications directly to the mothership. Her eyes twinkled. "Naturally," she smiled.

Hypnos rehydrated food as Ursula and Bopoto spoke. The astronauts shared a bland meal.

Over the coming days Europa sifted ever closer. The majority of their journey had been taken at lightening-speed; the crux of it was tediously slow. The astronauts were clamouring to escape their ship, to stretch their legs in the air of a (hopefully) hospitable atmosphere. A probe had long been sent ahead with androids to cordon off a section of the moon and terraform the atmosphere for their impeding arrival. The probe was unmanned, the robots incapable of communicating on a human level. The astronauts could only hope that they had succeeded in their mission.

Eventually the starship reached Europa. Jupiter II was dwarfed by its namesake, wreathed in the faded halo of Jupiter's ring system. Both planet and moon were intoxicating to behold. The astronauts spied several other moons nearby, though none were as striking as their temporary home.

Plans were made to descend to the surface. Their spaceship would remain in orbit, latching onto the gravitational pull of the moon to become a manmade satellite forevermore. It wouldn't be returning to the mothership. Hopefully, if all was well, the mothership would be coming to them.

The front-section of the starship broke away in two sections. One powered automatically towards Europa; the other blasted for a pre-determined area on Jupiter. Inside each was their temporary habitats, thought it was currently unknown whether the astronauts would ever make it to Jupiter. Five pods were then dispatched to Europa. Housed within each was a solitary astronaut and mounds of supplies.

The preemptive probe and its automated androids had done their job perfectly. Within a domed area of Europa air spiced with nitrogen, oxygen, argon, carbon dioxide, neon, helium and methane formed the basis of a mirror image of their home planet. Plants danced in a chilly breeze, and a rabbit or two scampered across fields of stark green grass.

Though their new home was on a distant star, the astronauts mimicked what they knew. They build the temporary habitat akin to a home back on Earth and ate a dinner of roasted rabbit, living there as human rather than Jovian.

Mimic pt. II

On a distant moon the five astronauts lived in a terraformed world as human. But dissent was growing amongst them. Some wanted to stick rigidly to their mission of first scoping out Europa, whilst some wanted to deviate and head straight for Jupiter. Arguments arose. Fighting erupted. And then five became three and two.

Qadir and Rafael remained on Europa. Adhering to their mission brief, they collected rock samples, recorded atmospheric levels outside of their terraformed dome, and searched for any forms of life-giving properties. The results were relayed back to the mothership, though it would be some time before they received a response.

Hypnos, Ursula and Bopoto headed down to Jupiter after modifying one of the pods. Bopoto opened her eyes onto the cold metal of the modified transporter, reality slipping and adjusting at the edges. She felt bad. As leader, it was her job to take command, and yet under her rule her team had dispersed. So far from home, with little comforts to console her, Bopoto slowly became unhinged. The long journey only amplified her annoyance.

The three astronauts descended beneath innumerable layers of gasses to reach the hidden core of Jupiter.

"Where's the base at?" Ursula asked, her voice muffled from her suit. She looked around. Jupiter wore a rocky landscape, ethereally wreathed in mist.

Bopoto shrugged.

"You don't know?" Ursula queried. Another shrug. "Well then turn your locator on." A further shrug. "What's wrong with you?"

"They're back up there!" Bopoto screamed, throwing her hand up in the general direction of Europa.

"It was their choice," Hypnos said. "They'll be down here before long anyway. I wouldn't worry."

"We're breaking protocol," Bopoto said, her voice cracking. "I thought they'd come with us straight away, when they knew we were leaving. We shouldn't have left them. We shouldn't have split."

"It doesn't matter," Ursula replied. There was a slight chuckle to her voice. "We're so far from the mothership. We're never returning. They can't do anything. By the time the mothership arrives, we'll be nearing death. It doesn't matter."

Ursula took charge then. She snatched Bopoto's locator and searched for the frequency of the habitat located on Jupiter. She stormed off. Hypnos swiftly followed. Bopoto trailed in their wake, lost within herself.

It took the three astronauts much longer to build the second habitat. Qadir was the builder within their group.

"What about the signal?" Hypnos asked one evening over a bland meal.

"It's still there," replied Ursula. She glanced at the locator. A shrill beep burst from it.

"We should check it out. I don't know why we're waiting."

"We're waiting for Qadir and Rafael," Bopoto mumbled.

"That could be weeks, months," Ursula said. "Oh, no, I don't want to wait. It took us long enough to get *here*."

"We're to go together. All of us."

"No!"

"Ladies," Hypnos said, trying to smooth everything out. He could feel the growing tension.

"I'm going." Ursula snatched up the locator.

"The hell you are!" Bopoto jumped to her feet.

"Try and stop me."

A fight broke out then. Hypnos left them to it. He headed outside and sent a message to Qadir and Rafael, asking them when they would be coming to Jupiter. By the time he received a response (*The reply from the mothership should be coming any day now, and then we'll be down*), the fight within had died out. Hypnos headed back inside.

Blood was smeared upon the walls. Ursula lay at Bopoto's feet.

"We can't even live together!" screeched Bopoto. "Five of us, and we can't even get on! What's gonna happen when the others come?"

"You killed her," was all Hypnos could say in response.

And then the signal sounded.

"They're coming," said Bopoto, looking over at the locator. "They're coming for us."

Their animosity fizzled out immediately. They forgot all about Ursula. Grabbing the locator, Hypnos and Bopoto headed out onto Jupiter in search of the aliens. That was why they had come, after all.

Mimic pt. III

On a distant world the two astronauts walked in silence. Anticipation joined them as a third. Both were scared; neither voiced their concerns.

Bopoto was the first to break the silence. "What do you think we'll find?" she asked. Both astronauts had completely forgotten the fact that Bopoto had recently killed one of their team. Their current objective was much too important - there would be time to mourn later.

Hypnos shrugged his shoulders. "I have no idea. Could be anything. Could be nothing at all."

"But the signal—"

"Doesn't mean aliens are causing it," Hypnos cut in. "I don't want to get my hopes up."

Silence fell over them again. They walked on.

Time passed. Their legs ached. And then the aliens appeared.

There was two of them. They stood in bipedal form, roughly the same height as a human. But their faces were far beyond comprehension. Mangled skin, stretched taut over cracked and protruding bones, leaked a greenish glowing liquid that seemed to sizzle in the air as it fell. Their eyes were squinted, matted in the green liquid so much that neither alien could see. Neither could speak. Nothing that resembled human speech, anyway.

But they mimicked the posture of a human. They both stood upright, though such stature seemed to cause them immeasurable pain. They walked on two legs; two arms hung limply either side. They groaned in pain, the only sound they could manage. To Hypnos it seemed as though they were desperately trying to communicate something.

Hypnos and Bopoto stopped short. A great intake of air rendered them both speechless.

Hypnos was the first to break it this time. "They can't talk."

"What were you expecting?" Bopoto countered.

"Not... not this." Words failed him. "Anything but this." He wasn't sure what he had even expected. Certainly not intellectual conversations about the meaning of life and the existence of the universe, but he had expected so much more than mute beings that looked to be on the verge of death. To him it would have been kinder to put them out of their misery. "What do we do with them?" he eventually asked.

"Do... with... them" Bopoto asked slowly. "I don't understand..."

"We need this world. We have to take it."

"Take it?"

"Yeah, take it. Take it from them! They might try to stop us. We need it."

"Do you honestly believe that? Look at them! They're barely alive! What are you even suggesting?"

"Euthanasia. It would be kinder than letting them live. They look like they're in pain. And anyway, more of us are coming - they'd be the only two of their kind. They'll be experimented on. Dissected. This would be kinder."

"Are you - you have to be kidding!"

"No." Hypnos stood stoically. "I'm the medic, after all," he said, as though this answered everything. "I've made up my mind. Are you going to stand in my way?"

Bopoto stood silently. She didn't know what to do.

"Are you?"

She readied herself. "What if I do?"

"Then you have to go too."

"*What?*"

"We need this world. Our people need this world. If I have to kill you along with them"—he jabbed a finger at the disfigured things before him—"so be it. Ending their miserable existence will mean that more of our people can thrive here." A slow tear trailed down his cheek. "I'm sorry."

He raised his gun. Three shots rang out.

*

Qadir and Rafael awaited the response from the mothership. They'd sent the results of their experiments to their counterparts back home. The reply should be coming any day now. Both were eager to journey to Jupiter and join their comrades, find out what they had missed.

As the reply arrived, a wormhole opened around their makeshift habitat. They had only seconds to act. Rafael sent out a distress signal to the mothership and then both astronauts were sucked inside.

They journeyed through space. Their signal was beamed through time.

When the wormhole opened once more Qadir and Rafael were close to death. Both were beyond recognition - broken grey skin, misshapen faces exuding a garish liquid. Neither could see. Neither could speak.

*

Five years ago their distress signal reached the mothership. And humanity listened.

*

Hypnos laughed as he looked down at the three corpses. It was only when his laughter died into crying that he realised he was alone. The aliens weren't aliens at all. It dawned on him that their suits were identical to his own. He didn't even near to read the ID tags to know that, somehow, he had killed Qadir and Rafael.

He fell to the floor and into insanity. His permeating moans mimicked the sound that the aliens had made.

Isolate

MISSION BRIEF

Earth is in ruin. The remnants of humanity cling to destitute hopes of salvation, camped out on a distant moon that supports extraterrestrial vegetation and wildlife. All that humanity see is food for survival. The bland ball has been terraformed, but an exoplanet is required for continual existence. The moon can only last for so long. A band of survivors embark on their most dangerous mission to date: isolating themselves for a year. Only then will they know whether humanity can survive in harsher habitats. Only then will they know whether humanity has any hope of continuing or not.

MISSION STATUS

Isolation officially aborted. All members deceased—

I guess I've always felt isolated.

*

Palm trees sway in a breeze that I cannot feel. Their coconuts clack with a sound I cannot hear. The salt spray stings the air but I cannot taste it. I am isolated. Cut off from the world by a great glass dome of segregation. We are isolated through choice, though I'm growing to regret that decision. Everything is necessary, though.

*

Peeling back the metal lid, the stench of humanity hits me square in the face. It's the smell of tinned tuna that stings my sensitive nostrils, really, but it's humanity that preserved that tuna and humanity that produced the tin can. I can smell fish, but all I can think of is humanity. Oh, how I miss humanity.

And I miss food too. Real food, I mean. Not this tuna. After having it every day for the past ten weeks, I've grown to really hate tuna. Tuna. I'm isolated with tuna. And I feel sick.

It's all I have to eat, though, so I have to force myself to chew methodically. I retch as I chew, but I chew regardless. This is my meal. My isolated meal.

*

"What's for tea?" Simmons says.

"Tuna," I reply, bored. This has become a joke between us. A joke that I grimace at when I deliver the punchline. "Tuna for tea."

"I'm sure I spotted some anchovies earlier," Chapman chimes in. "Or sardines. I forget which." Chapman doesn't mind the relentless barrage of tuna. For now he can't get enough. But he'll grow to hate it, I know he will. He'll grow to empathise with us.

"Where?" Simmons and I ask in unison. We both whip around to stare hungrily at him.

Chapman shrugs his shoulders. "On the database. Don't you remember?"

"Remember?" I ask. "Remember what?"

"We put some aside months ago, when our stores were depleting. We put some aside for a rainy day."

I look through the great glass dome. Rain hammers interminable against the dome, echoing like mocking applause all around. It's most definitely a rainy day today.

"Where?" I ask again. "Show me!"

"Jesus, Kim, calm down," Chapman responds.

"We don't speak of such religions in the dome," Hudson sternly reminds us all.

"Sorry," Chapman mumbles. "I forget myself sometimes. Sorry."

"That's all right," says Hudson. "You just have to try and remember."

"I don't even believe in Christianity." Chapman feels the need to explain himself. I can tell. He's talking animately, and his arms are floundering all around. "Never have. It's a dying religion, but its deities remain vigil. The deities of all those old religions do. And, I like cussing."

"Just try to remember," Hudson says again, and that's that.

I watch the to-and-fro listlessly. I care nothing of their religious preaching. "Show me the database," I say again. I feel positively religious with my determination to find the anchovies or sardines.

With a flurry of clicking, Chapman opens the database. He scrolls down the spreadsheet.

"We've never spoken of religion before," Chapman says as he scrolls. "I just realised."

"It doesn't matter," Ahmed says.

"Whatever religion we follow remains out there," Hudson intones, nodding his head at the dome. "In here we're isolated from it all."

"But we can talk of it, yeah? We're allowed to talk of it."

A terse pause greets him. I can tell Hudson would like nothing more than to lie to him. But he cannot. He must be truthful. "Yes," he finally concedes. "We are free to talk of religion."

Chapman smiles broadly. His eyes never leave the screen. "So, anyone religious?"

A wall of silence greets him. Finally:

"I am," Ahmed says.

"Which religion do you follow?"

"Neo-Hinduism."

"Never heard of it," Chapman shrugs. "That a new one?"

"Fairly, yes. It follows most of the same traction as Hinduism of old."

"Why's it called *Neo*-Hinduism then?"

"All new religions are."

"Fair enough." Chapman shrugs again. "Anyone else?"

Another wall of silence greets him. "No?" Chapman says. "Fair enough. I am."

"You're religious?" Ahmed asks incredulously.

"Yes."

"What religion do you follow?"

"Zephyric."

"*Zephyric?*"

"Yes."

"But—"

"He's free to believe in what he wants to believe in," Hudson cuts in. He, like me, can sense a growing animosity between the two men.

"I know, but—"

"Be careful in what you say next, Ahmed," Hudson warns.

"It's alright," says Chapman. "He can say what he wants. I can take it. I face animosity wherever I go."

"This is why I think religion should be one of the codas we're forbidden to discuss," Hudson says. "There's too much animosity."

"It's alright," Chapman says again. He clicks onto the next page of the database.

"The Zephyr wiped out our planet," Ahmed says.

"Our *ancestor's* planet," Chapman corrects him. A smile of sickly serenity spreads his lips.

"Okay, fair enough - our ancestor's planet. But they still wiped it out, took the majority of humanity with it, too. You think that's alright?"

"Yes."

"What the fu—"

"I don't think I know what themes Zephyric follows," Simmons muses.

"It's quite similar to Hinduism of old," Chapman notes. "The prevalent themes include karma and samsara. The Zephyr decimated Earth because of our continued exploration of planets that didn't belong to Earth. That was karma. What goes around, comes around. But humanity has been reborn and aims to try again, thus: samsara, the cycle of death and rebirth. It really is a quite peaceful religion. You'd do well to research it a little before you condemn me for my beliefs." Chapman finally looks up from the screen. His eyes burn as he looks at Ahmed. "All I'm saying is this: the Zephyr came and killed humanity, but that was generations ago. 100 years. Whoever they killed in your family, you would never have met anyway. It makes no difference."

"Makes no difference?" Ahmed repeats.

"Maybe my phrasing was wrong."

"Yes, I think it was."

"I don't follow the religions of old, simply because they no longer have any footing in our reborn society. I say *Jesus* as an expletive, but I don't believe in Christianity. How can I? The son of God was reborn upon a planet that no longer exists. How can I follow a religion whose origins no longer exist?"

"That's why we have Neo-Christianity, Neo-Hinduism, Neo —"

"Fair enough," Chapman says. "But Neo-Christianity isn't Christianity. It can't be. I believe in what I know, and I *know* that the Zephyr are real. Like Hudson said: believe in what you want to believe in. I hold no animosity towards you with regards to what you believe in. Nor should you."

"This is all well and good," I say, the words spilling from my trembling lips with dripping disconcertion, "but all I care about right now are those anchovies and sardines. Have you found them yet?"

*

The anchovies aren't anchovies. Not really. The alien fish were harvested, preserved and canned on this moon, but they look remarkably like anchovies of Earth. That's why we call them anchovies. Same with the tuna.

But I don't care.

All I care about is that I don't have to eat tuna today. Today I have anchovies. I no longer feel isolated. We are happy with our anchovies, eating them in our segregated society.

*

"Anyone seen Ahmed?"

I look up and shake my head.

"I've not seen him for a few hours," Hudson says.

"His tracker will be on," Chapman points out. "Go have a look."

I watch Hudson cross to his computer terminal as I apply my lipstick. I check it in the mirror. I'm beginning to look like myself. Beginning to *feel* like myself.

"He's not there," Hudson says, a trace of worry in his tones.

"Not where?" Quinn asks.

I rub the gel between my hands as I look to Hudson.

"Not anywhere," comes Hudson's reply.

"But he has to be," I say.

I slick the gel through my hair, peeling it back from my forehead. I turn to Simmons. He seems to read my mind.

"Want a hand?"

"Please."

So Simmons helps me apply the skull cap. I pin it in place as Chapman joins Hudson at the terminal.

"There must be a problem with his tracker."

"Kim, a hand? You're the computer whizkid, after all."

"In a second," I reply. "I'm almost ready."

I wash my hands, feeling the gel sluice off of them, before pulling the black wig from its protective wrappings. I'll brush it when it's applied. But for now all I want is for it to be on. Then I'll truly be myself.

Chapman rolls his eyes. Hudson notices this. I do too.

"I saw that," Hudson says.

"Saw what?"

"You roll your eyes."

"And?"

"Prejudices remain outside," Hudson reminds him. "Just like religion."

"I didn't bring my bigotry inside," Chapman retorts. His words cut like diamonds.

"You rolled your eyes."

"Yeah, because we're missing a guy, and all that faggot over there can do is dress up like a woman."

"Hey, that's unfair!" Quinn shouts out immediately.

"You can't say things like that!" Simmons says.

"Chapman," Hudson warns. "You simply *cannot* say stuff like. It's forbidden."

"All I'm saying is we have more pressing matters to attend to."

Tears sting at my eyes but I refuse to let them flow. I've spent too long on my makeup, and I've faced prejudice before. I'll face it again. I always will. Even the remnants of humanity clinging desperately to survival cannot live in harmony. People will always tear others apart based on preconceived notions of sexuality, gender, religion, class. The list is endless. But I've faced it all before. I've always felt isolated.

So I stand up. I'm going to be the bigger person here. The bigger woman. Because that's how I feel. I feel like a woman. Fuck him. Fuck Chapman and his transphobic ways. Fuck everyone that feels that way.

I don't look at him as I reach his terminal. I refuse to give him the pleasure of my dissatisfaction. I access the tracking programme and see five blue dots blinking on the computerised layout of the dome structure, five dots that are in the main hub. But there are six of us.

"He's not there," I say.

"That what *I* said!" Chapman says through gritted teeth. He drums his fingers on the tabletop, incessantly so.

I run a hand through my hair. The wig feels more natural than the hair beneath. "Give me a second," I reply airily. "I can find him."

I patch into Ahmed's network, meaning that the entire computer system is tuned into looking for him. Every sensor in the dome in searching. Every camera is mapping a projected destination based on his prior movements. Every record of his activities are being crosschecked with these conjured destinations.

A sixth dot finally lights up, alongside 5 words.

Only this dot is red. We're all blue.

*

"What are you doing?"

I look up from my tuna to see Quinn confronting Chapman.

"Praying," Chapman says.

"Don't. He wasn't Zephyric."

"I am."

"Yeah, but he wasn't. Don't isolate him in his death. Don't pray to a God he didn't believe in. Don't pray for him."

"I can do what the hell I want." Chapman's voice has turned into a growl.

"No, you can't," Hudson says. He wanders over and stands between the two men. "Religion remains outside. You're forbidden to pray."

"But *that's* isolating *me*."

"You knew what you signed up for."

I chew autonomously as I watch the fight. It's the third fight this morning. The seventh since we found Ahmed's disembowelled body.

"Well I quit. I want out."

"You can't, though, I agree. This mission should come to an end. But it's impossible. The dome remains closed for a year. We have another one hundred and fifty seven days of isolation."

*

It's going to be a long one hundred and fifty seven days.

*

"*Gotwad will consume us all*," Simmons reads from the computer terminal. Those are the words that appeared alongside Ahmed's red dot. "What do you think they mean?"

Nobody has an answer.

*

I want this mission to be over. Not so that I can escape this dome, not so that we can prove to the survivors that we can survive in harsh climates, no. I want this mission to be over so that I can finally transition. I heard this morning that I've reached the top of the waiting list.

Only one hundred and forty days left.

*

"Is it like Ahmed?"

I nod my head.

"Exactly the same?"

I nod my head again. I can't muster the words.

"When?"

I swallow hard. I can feel my stomach churning, regurgitating last nights tuna. "Some time last - last night. I can't be certain until I run diagnostics. We'll have to get it back to the main lab."

I refuse to label the body as 'he'. I refuse to name the body as 'Simmons'. Only then will it make it real. Until then it's just a second body. A John Doe. Until then we're still five members, not an isolated four.

"Help me carry it back."

"No."

Hudson places a hand on my shoulder and I look up, bemused.

"No," he says again. "We'll get Quinn. He can help carry it. This is no job for a woman."

Despite the gravitas of the situation I smile. Hudson is a true gentleman. He treats me as I am. A woman.

"Thank you," I reply.

"Don't sweat it."

*

"We have ninety seven days left," Hudson says to the isolated quartet. "Ninety seven days to prove that we can survive. And two of us haven't. I guess," he adds slowly, "that Gotwad consumed them. Whatever that means."

"I've been running scans on the surveillance," I say, my voice timid. "And I think I know how they died. Or rather, who killed them. I think I know who Gotwad is. I wasn't sure whether I should say anything, but... it has to stop. I don't want to be next."

My heart is pumping furiously and I refuse to look my colleagues in the eye. I refuse to look at the murderer. But it must be said. He must be isolated from us all, lest he picks us off one by one. Finally, I name him.

"Chapman."

"What?" Quinn rounds on him instantly. His fist is raised.

"What the fuck are you on about?" Chapman growls. He takes a step towards me, but Quinn punches him.

"No."

"You fucking faggot! I never killed anyone." Chapman sidesteps Quinn and grabs my arm. I try to pull away but Chapman manages to pull me towards him.

Hudson pushes him away. Ever the gentlemen.

I cower away and access the surveillance on my computer terminal. "Chapman exits the hub both times. He returns *after* the death has been carried out. It's the only logical explanation. We've logged no technological issues, and it was only ever the six of us in the compound. We've long suspected that it was one of us that was killing off the crew. It *has* to be Chapman."

"You fairy! You fucking—"

"Lock him away."

Hudson stands his ground.

*

"It wasn't me!"

We three look at him. He is isolated in his cell. He growls at us from between the bars that imprison him.

"I didn't kill anyone! You have no proof!"

"If it wasn't you," Hudson says, "then who was it?"

"I don't know. I don't know. I don't - it wasn't me! You have to believe me."

I toss him a tin of tuna.

We leave him isolated.

*

"You're in charge."

I stare.

"Did you hear me, Kim? You're in charge. Commander Priapus Kim. Unless, that is, you've chosen your new name?"

I continue to stare.

Quinn shakes me by the shoulder.

"Kim?"

"Uh, yeah. Aphroditus. That is what I want to be known as. Aphroditus."

"Commander Aphroditus Kim."

"Why me?"

"You're higher up than me."

"But Chapman…"

"We voted. We both chose you."

"Even *Chapman*?"

"Even Chapman."

I shiver. "What do we do now?"

"You're the Commander. You have to decide."

I look down at Hudson's mangled corpse, awash in a sea of blood. His remains are mangled beyond recognition. "Release Chapman. It wasn't him. I was wrong. We have thirty nine days of survival left. Nobody should be isolated. We need unity. We need strength. We need to survive."

*

My last meal will consist of tuna.

Big surprise.

*

"How did they die?"

"It wasn't any of us," I reply. I look at Chapman. There's a newfound respect for one another that seems to have arisen from nowhere.

"So if it wasn't us… who was it? These marks can't be from some technological breakdown. They were inflicted by a person. Or, rather, some form of sentience. Picking us off one by one. Isolating us."

"Gotwad," says Quinn.

"You think there's someone else in here with us?" I ask.

"Or some*thing,*" Chapman replies.

We shiver in unison. We are united. No longer isolated.

"But what?"

"I don't know." I look around. Goosebumps erect the hairs on my arms, like the tender limbs of arachnids stretching as they scurry to and fro. I shiver.

"Search for all signs of life," Quinn says. "*All* signs of life. Artificial. Cold blooded. Disembodied sentience. Even robotic. There has to be some signs."

I quickly do as Quinn instructed me. The computer searches for all signs of life.

"It'll take a few minutes," I say.

"What do we do in the meantime?" Chapman asks.

"Eat?" Quinn suggests. "I'm sure there's a tin or two of tuna around here." He grins as he wanders from the room.

I look to Chapman.

The computer beeps.

A scream rents the air, before silence eclipses everything.

*

We never did get to eat that last tin of tuna.

Whatever is ensconced in the dome with us picked off Quinn before we had our last meal.

It's just me and Chapman now.

Isolated.

Alone.

*

"What do we do?" Chapman asks. Fear threads through his voice, wavering his vocal cords. He looks to me as a captain.

"We have twenty one hours left," I say. "So far, whatever is here with us has remained hidden. It only showed up on the computer when I scanned for cold blooded creatures. It kills at night and seventeen of our remaining hours are during the day time. I say we lock ourselves in the prison cells and stay there. It's the only way we'll make it out of this alive. Agreed?"

Chapman swallows hard. I get the impression he's fighting the involuntary impulse to be sick. Finally he nods.

*

I lock the door to the prison and we settle in for the long slog of banality. Just the two of us. We're getting on now, but I cannot and will not forgive Chapman for his transphobic comments. Likewise, the hatred for who I am simmers behind his dark eyes, and I know that this animosity is mutual. But it is just the two of us. We have to be civil. We have to survive.

As I pull open a tin of tuna the lights above crackle and blink.

"Power's on the fritz," Chapman says, stating the obvious.

"Not long left," I say. "We'll make it."

Through the dome above us the sky is blackened. Not a single star tarnishes the stretch of nothingness. The moon we reside on is isolate.

The lights plunge us into darkness, and a scratching permeates the suffering silence.

"What was that?" I ask.

"It's out there. Whatever it is - it's out there! Do you hear it? Scratching. Trying to get in. And it will."

Chapman's facade of cool indifference drops and in that instance he loses his mind.

"Come on, there's another way out of here," I say. I take his hand, but he cringes away. He cannot bare to feel my skin upon his own. "Are you serious?" I ask incredulously.

"I... I..."

"Fuck you. Fuck you and die." The venom in my voice is palpable. "That thing - whatever it is - seems to feed and then hibernate for a while. That's why there was so much time between each death. It all makes sense. Fuck you. I'll live."

I turn and run for the faraway door.

I lock it before Chapman even knows what has happened.

On the other side I hear the first door slowly creak open.

The alien, Gotwad - whatever it is - is in there with Chapman.

*

I am isolated.

*

I guess I've always felt isolated.

*

The alien stalks down the corridor. I'm ready.

I strike out the moment it enters my field of view, barely taking in its shining hide of toughened skin, or its wide intelligent eyes. I care nothing for what it looks like. All I want is for it to die.

The axe hits a pipe and a jet of vapour issues, creating an artificial miasma all around. The alien cowls away, pining in pain.

I strike out again. And again. And again.

Blood streams across the floor, only this time it's not human blood.

I turn and run.

*

Ten.

Nine.

Eight.

Seven.

Six.

Five.

Four.

Three.

Two.

One.

The door slowly creaks open and for the first time in exactly a year I feel the cool air of the hostile moon upon my skin. It's the best feeling.

I escape the dome and my year of isolation, leaving the bodies of my colleagues and the alien hunter behind. I steal away into the night, never looking back.

I'll never see another human face again, I know, though I'll escape the moon and prosper. But that's alright. I'm good at being alone. I'm good at being isolated. I am a free woman.

*

MISSION STATUS

Isolation officially aborted. All members deceased. No signs of life. Insanity reigned and they picked one another off.

In The Desert

In the desert time does not exist.

In the desert the slightest of whispering winds amplifies into an endless vacuum of dead air.

In the desert rocks break and roll and change.

In the desert sand is all around.

In the desert day turns into night and night into day.

In the desert everything changes slowly but nothing is there to witness.

In the desert beauty is all around.

In the desert stars twinkle above and lava broils beneath.

In the desert life is nonexistent.

In the desert the rockets land—

"Gotwad Will Consume Us All"

Minerva Kim stole away into the night.

A full orb cast its ethereal ghostly hue upon the castle. She traced the moon with rabid eyes. Behind, she spied the second. Rain fell all around, each droplet carrying a slip of moonlight so bright that it appeared as though a waterfall of twinkling lights blinked alluringly around, allowed Minerva to fleetingly forget her fear, and her inquisition. Their mesmerising movements momentarily took her limited concentration; she was transfixed by their beauty.

But then the preternatural prophecy recurred in her mind, drawing her to the present.

"Gotwad will consume us all."

She shivered in the rain and hurried on her way. Lightning laughed manically all around.

The catacombs of the towering castle existed as a gateway between Minerva and Gotwad. They were policed by shapeshifting beings that cantered from human to wolf form in the blink of an eye, whilst cackling potion brewers excelled at casting illusionary spells all around. Lumbering grotesque creations conjured from Gotwad's perverse mind laboured around, grunting incoherently. They shone sickly green, clawing for brain matter. Gotwad's playthings prowled the vaults, puppets to his whims.

Minerva navigated the labyrinthine maze of twisting corridors and narrow passageways until she arrived at an ancient door. It seemed to sigh when she opened it, as its rusty hinges moaned in pain or pleasure - she could not decipher the sounds, though they elicited a horror of horripilation down her forearms.

A barren, abandoned room greeted her. A disused laboratory. She stepped timorously inwards.

The room was dark and cold, though a crackling torch up ahead threw shadows all around, shadows that danced painstakingly close. Minerva stalled in her steps as fear threatened to overtake her, but she repeated the prophecy aloud to remind her of her goal: "Gotwad will consume us all."

At the far end of the room a sepulchre awaited Minerva, where ten cadaverous shapes loomed out of the darkness. The slaves of Gotwad had been stuffed and preserved before death, meaning that they held their shapes perfectly. Eerily so.

"Gotwad will consume us all," Minerva repeated for the third time, as if to remind herself why she had ventured on a suicidal mission. Her voice echoed, giving the impression that the ten stuffed bodies were whispering along with her. Minerva felt goose pimples map fear onto her arms. She felt as though she was disturbing something that ought not be disturbed. But she knew she must persevere.

She carried onto the antechamber and fainted.

*

Minerva came around to the faint whisperings of a ghost.

"Gotwad will consume us all," the pale figure said. Minerva could see through the apparition. It resembled the form of Poseidon, with flowing locks and scarlet eyes. Minerva felt a stirring at the sight. Oh, how she missed Poseidon. Gotwad had consumed him. She had loved him dearly. "Gotwad will consume us all," Poseidon said again, "and anarchy will reign. Humanity will be snuffed out and Gotwad will prevail. He must be stopped at all costs."

At the far end of the room Minerva glimpsed a shadow that took on her form; a second flitted into the form of Gotwad. Glistening fangs hung below his bottommost lip, and his intelligent eyes were rimmed in red. He stared hungrily at the shadowy silhouette of Minerva.

They're dancing, Minerva thought. *We're dancing.*

But her nebulous counterpart lunged forward and, when she stepped back, a wooden dagger pierced Gotwad's chest. He stumbled and fell, and the prophetic ghost laughed aloud. "You will kill him. You will *consume* Gotwad."

Minerva's eyes flittered daintily as the ghost cackled, and she succumbed to unconsciousness once more.

*

Sometime later, Minerva came to her senses. Darkness crept around the room, throwing shadows into stark relief. Outside rain continued to fall in an unrelenting waterfall, and the wind of the surrounding valleys whispered incoherently. To Minerva they seemed to whisper the never-ending prophecy.

Gotwad.

Everything came back to Gotwad. And it was down to Minerva to end the plight of her people, to end the nightly massacres and feasts of blood.

Slowly she stood. Before her, in the antechamber, a cove of extraterrestrial babies cooed, their eyes shot with red. None had teeth, yet, but they all looked at her with the intelligence that Gotwad exuded. Ten babies stared hungrily up at her, and Minerva felt her blood run cold. They sought her for sustenance, she knew.

"Ah," a voice said from behind her.

Minerva whipped round, the skirts of her dress swishing. A man stood before her, half-basked in shadows.

"Who- who are you?" Minerva timorously asked.

The man smiled thinly. "I am... your nightmare. I am your dream." He took a step forward.

"My... my... I'm not sure I under- understand."

"And nor shall you," the man said. "But come, you must be so cold. Come to the warmth."

The man stepped quickly past Minerva, so quickly that Minerva failed to make out any distinguishable feature of his face. He stepped to a roaring fire that Minerva had hitherto failed to see, and it was only then that Minerva realised how cold she truly was. The hairs on her arms stood erect with fear. Slowly, she passed the gawking babies and followed the unknown man to her fate.

"Those... those bab- those things back there"—Minerva glanced back to the babies, and was unsurprised to find all ten were watching them avidly—"what are they?" Minerva's teeth chattered - whether from coldness or fear she could not tell. Maybe it was both.

"Why, they're my children," the man replied.

"Your ch- ch- children?"

"Yes." The man's voice floated upon the air, serpentining towards Minerva, and Minerva took an innate step backwards.

"I... don't..."

"And nor shall you," the man said once more, cutting Minerva off. He finally stepped from the shadows. His eyes were scarlet, and his lips extended into a predatory smile. He was remarkably beautiful, with a shining hide as pale as the lunar surface of the maddening moons up above.

"You- you're Gotwad."

It wasn't a question. Minerva knew it to be true. Her eyes rolled into the back of her head and she passed out once more.

*

She came around in Gotwad's arms. The alien caressed her cheek as he drank from Minerva, his lips slurping and his tongue lolling. Minerva felt no pain; all she felt was arousal. Gotwad had elicited unbidden desires within Minerva, and Minerva all too willingly entered his embrace.

Gotwad had freed her. Gotwad had consumed her.

*

She played the waiting game for a long time. Pretending to be in agreement with Gotwad, the alien parasite slowly opened up to Minerva and told her of his plans, his plans to journey across the vast desert and consume the humans that were waiting in their metal strongholds. Food, he said, that would last them until the end of time. There may even be leftovers for the children.

Minerva humoured him. Minerva fed him. Minerva did his every whim. And when he slept she worked. She still feared the babies, and skirted the outside of the chamber when passing them, but she knew they couldn't tell Gotwad what she was doing.

She, like her ancestral predecessors, had volunteered for a suicide mission. It was in her blood, the need to ensure the survival of those that came after. And she was desperate to secure her daughter's life. That was why she lit the torch.

Flames licked through the castle in an instant. Gotwad's playthings cowled in darkness that was suddenly lit from within; skin burned quickly from their bodies and their eyes popped garishly. The walls began to crumble. The children cried in fear and Minerva smiled at their distress. She didn't have time to escape. She sat, ensconced on Gotwad's throne, and observed the destruction.

"You... You..."

Minerva looked round. Gotwad stalked towards her, his eyes wide with fury. The whites reflected the flames and in that instant they were overcome with redness. But then the flames licked at Gotwad's fur and he howled.

"You..."

Gotwad lunged at Minerva, his mind alive with death, as the collapsing castle consumed them both.

The Narcissist

It shifted in a warm embrace and then stilled for an indeterminable length of time. Then it shifted once more. It stopped and started until it split, caring nothing for anything bar itself.

The first crack was small. Barely noticeable. But a grain penetrated the shell and the entity within writhed uncomfortably. It was cramped inside, and the grain took up valuable space. The writhing amplified the predetermined and carefully orchestrated plan, and the crack lengthened. A second forked off, and soon a spiderwebbing system of ruts ran across the entire surface.

A segment of the shell broke away entirely not long after, and the entity roused its infantile head. It pushed out, twisting this way and that, looking. Always looking.

But it was never sated, and it continued its exploration. The elongated neck followed next, pushing the head onwards. The entity continued burrowing. First it went down, then to the left, before realising that these were the wrong ways entirely. It span its entire form around and headed upwards. Up and up. Pushing past a mass of grains until it broke free.

Sunlight streamed upon the lavender ground as the tiny seedling first appeared. A minuscule dot of green. Nothing more. And there it waited.

Sun. Rain. Night. Sun. Rain. Night. Sun. Rain. Night.

On and on.

The monotony of its days rolled onwards but within the sequence of warmth and wetness and darkness the seedling found its strength growing, and that was all it sought. Strength for itself, to continue its journey into maturity.

As time rolled on the seedling grew into its teenage years. There it vegetated, bored and lazy. It blew in the wind but barely continued looking around. It no longer cared. Pubic leaves burst as it grew in length. And then came its sexual awakening: the first bud arose.

Then it cared.

It craned its neck, seeking the empowering sun up above, craving its warmth. As it craned, its neck stretched, and the flower continued to grow. Mature. Develop.

The bud suddenly cracked open, releasing a spore of hypnotic pollen that attracted bees. They buzzed incessantly around, drifting forward for a smell before darting off to copulate. The hornets were the worst: they hovered around, barely interacting. Their drone was deafening.

The roots grew, too, foraging beneath the ground on the hunt for water droplets. They became razor-sharp, stretching and stretching. On and on.

And finally the narcissus spread its alluring petals wide and relaxed into maturity. White petals danced in the ruffling breeze whilst a core of molten yellow sent an arousing scent into the fresh air. But the flower cared nothing for the wildlife it attracted, or for its neighbouring plants or the humans that watched its progress in awe. It cared only for itself. The narcissus lived up to its name: it was narcissistic.

I Would Give Everything, or: All The Things I Never Said

"I never told you how much I loved you."

Aphroditus Kim studied her father's gnarled face. He looked ancient, and had aged considerably in the 6 years since she had first left to enter the isolation dome. He was bald, his pate shining beneath the setting sun, and his face was lined in wrinkles. His jaw was adorned in a scraggly beard of white wisps. But when he smiled his entire face lit up; his eyes sparkled. The wrinkles momentarily vacated as the smile stretched the skin.

Ares Kim shook his head. "Aphro—"

"I never told you how much you mean to me. You or dad."

The smile vanished. His brow creased into a frown that added years to his age and it looked to Aphroditus that he was in pain.

"I knew," her father said. "We both knew. You didn't need to say a thing. All you needed to do was be you."

Aphroditus felt uncomfortable. She was regretting this conversation already.

"Did he say anything to you? When I left, I mean."

"Just how proud of you he was. He kept telling me that he missed you. That he hoped you were okay."

"And when he—" Aphroditus' voice momentarily faltered. She felt tears brimming in the corners of her eyes and she hastily blinked them away. "When he died. Did he say anything then?"

"He told me he missed his daughter."

Daughter.

A tear fell now; Aphroditus couldn't help it. Her parents had accepted her entirely, she knew that already, but she still craved the acknowledgement like a baby craved the nipple.

"He was devastated that he didn't get to see you one last time."

Aphroditus took a swallow of synthetic gin, grimacing as it burned at her throat. She still marvelled at the fact that one of the first things humanity had done upon colonising an alien world was to craft alcohol. The burn helped her control her tears.

"He kept mumbling your name. Your old name, I mean. I wish he could see you now. You truly are beautiful."

Aphroditus thought otherwise. Her sole wig was tattered and her thin, slightly-malnourished face was painted grotesquely with watered sands and dirts. She sought femininity; she was presented as a savage. But there was nothing she could do and, really, it didn't much matter. Her father was the only human she was ever going to see again and in his eyes she was beautiful.

"You look so confident. You look so proud of who you are, of what you've endured. I know you don't like to talk about it, about your time there, but it's changed you, I can tell. For the better? Maybe. It's certainly not a bad thing."

Another tear fell. "I would give everything... *everything*... to go back," she choked.

Ares snatched up one of her hands and looked her squarely in the face. "Why?" The pained look was back and, for a brief interlude, he, too, looked like he was on the verge of crying.

"To see him one last time. To see you both, happy and healthy. To tell you both how much you mean to me. All the things I never said. Now it's too late."

They fell into silence. They watched, from afar, as tens of thousands of their people quarried the desert of TRAPPIST-1e like ants searching for food. They were building new homes and farms. Faraway Aphroditus spied a field of flowers, the first of many experiments they had undertaken on this alien world to ensure it was completely hospitable. Again, she marvelled. She felt proud of her people, of their accomplishments. They had never given up; she couldn't, either.

"Come on," she said, her voice choked. "We need to go for a ride."

Aphroditus remembered the time she had shared water with her fathers after they had buried her grandmother. All she had ever wanted was to have a drink with her dads. A pint. A right of passage... Something that would never come to fruition. She took another mouthful of gin, her face contorting in agony as it sloshed down her throat like acid rain. She thrust the half-empty bottle into the passenger seat and took the helm. The small pod, the craft that she and her fellow Isolates had flown to the dome, rose slowly. For a brief moment the horrors of that ordeal washed over her and the pod plummeted as she lost control. The terraformed landscape, the palm trees, the faux-tuna, the bodies and the beast... She closed her eyes and breathed deeply.

"Hey." Her father's hand on her arm was warm and comforting. "You okay?"

"Yeah," Aphroditus murmured, "just... memories."

"What are you thinking about?"

The pod continued to rise. Beneath, the ground receded, the people becoming nothing more than dots and then... nothing.

"That place. That dome."

"Do you want to talk about it?"

After a moment's pause, Aphroditus nodded. "I suppose. Now would be the best time, I guess."

"What happened to you up there?" Her father seemed to breathe the words; they came soft and barely audible.

"There was something with us. In the dome. It picked us off, one-by-one." Aphroditus looked through the window. "We're not alone here. There's other life in this solar system. Is that a good thing? Maybe. Depends. Depends whether that life means us harm or not."

Ares nodded. "We've already encountered some. Your aunt... she sacrificed herself to put a stop to it. We were being attacked, killed, eaten, abducted. We only ever saw one of... whatever it was. And Minerva - she went to it. I don't know how she did it, but she did. She killed the beast, that *vastly* intelligent beast, and everything looks alright now. I mean, you saw for yourself. You saw our people denuding desert in order to build a new home. Maybe that's the end of it. Maybe not. But we have to be optimistic. And if there is other life here, other *hostile* life... well, we're just gonna have to work out a way to live in harmony. United."

Aphroditus looked at her father as the pod shot across the dark vista of space. It was on automatic, so she didn't need to pilot. Around her, scores of stars blurred as the pod picked up speed, and the occasional chunk of rock blasted by. A trio of planets loomed up before them: red, blue, green. One was a desert world, one was awash in water, one was consumed by vegetation. Everything that humanity needed to live peacefully here. And, with the rockets, travel from one planet to another was entirely possible. All that stood in their way was themselves - humanity would have to work together in order to prosper. From the stories Aphroditus had heard from her father's home world, she wasn't entirely sure that feat was possible.

"This... thing. Did you see it?"

Aphroditus already suspected what the thing was. Gotwad. She had left it alive in the dome; of course it had chased after humanity, having already got a taste for it.

"Briefly," her father replied. "It only ever came at night, so of course it was dark. What I remember the most is its eyes - wide, white... intelligent. It was a beast alright, a mighty predator, but it sure knew what it was doing."

Aphroditus bowed her head in acknowledgement. That sounded like Gotwad alright.

"It chanted. That's how we knew it was coming. It chanted a word, a word that we came to believe was its name. That's what we dubbed it anyway."

"And what... what was the word?" Aphroditus breathed, fearing the answer.

"Gotwad."

Goosebumps erupted across Aphroditus' arms like minuscule volcanos, burning her flesh with fear.

"But you said... Aunt Minerva... she killed it. Right?"

"That's what we think, yes," Ares replied. "It had a lair in the desert. We saw an explosion. That thing never returned. We can only pray that Minerva was successful."

They fell into silence again as the red planet grew closer.

"Why are we heading here?" Ares asked.

"You know why."

"But... I don't want to. I want to stay here, with you."

Was that fear? Aphroditus was certain her father's vocal cords quivered. She looked over at him. "We have to go."

"No we don't. We can continue what we've been doing - travelling the solar system. I want to explore the jungles - let's head to the green planet."

Aphroditus shook her head. The pod descended through the atmosphere of the red planet and the desert swam up to greet them. The destination was pre-programmed; they had been there before.

"Come on, Aphroditus," Ares whispered. "Let's go. We don't need to come here. We don't need to do this. We could do anything, anything at all, but this. Not this."

She definitely heard fear in his voice. He was rambling, his words rushing and merging together in confusion. But she didn't respond. If she did, she knew she might falter.

The pod landed, crunching against the rock-covered ground. Aphroditus wore a mask of indifference as she stood. She refused to cry. She looked out at the graveyard of cairns.

She took hold of a scrap of metal that would serve as her shovel, and began to dig her father's grave. Her father stood watching. He was silent now. He let her work.

"There's so much I should have said to you. So I'm going to say it now - all the things I never said. Maybe you'll hear it, maybe you won't, but I want you to know that I love you and I miss you already. I don't know how I'm going to cope. You've been my everything. You've helped me more than you probably realise. Simply by being you. By loving me. By accepting me for who I am. For not trying to change me. For pushing me to do what I wanted. For being proud. For being... my dad." Her voice choked. Tears began to fall, moistening her dry face. She took a pause from her dig to drink a hearty swallow of gin, relishing the burn now. Just to feel something. "That's my biggest regret. I don't regret going into isolation and I don't regret waiting so long to live my truth. I just regret not having the chance to tell you everything I should have. Huh." Aphroditus expelled a short laugh, a hollow laugh, one void of humour. "You know what's funny? We're all part of a legacy and I never fully appreciated that until this moment. I'm a Kim. I've had a hell of a lot to live up to and, y'know... I think I managed that. I think I managed to live up to the legacy of the Kims. I think I managed to live up to you and dad."

Aphroditus stepped from the shallow grave, tears streaming down her face in black trails as they washed away her poor attempt at femininity.

In that moment a sense of tranquility overcame her. She sat in the lip of the grave, her father's body wrapped in shawls behind her, and drank the remainder of the gin. Slowly, pride crept across her body and she managed to sniff away the tears. She lay a hand on the body. "I made you proud, didn't I?" As she spoke, her eyes wandered to the nearby cairn that signposted her other dad's body. "And... you know what? I'm proud, too. I am. I'm proud to be a Kim."

The Chronicles of Kim

The remnants of humanity basked in their legacy. The stories were passed from mouth to mouth so that all knew, even those that came afterwards. All knew of Earth and of the English Space Agency, of Armstrong's pioneering journey into space, of the Kims that went beyond. The stories became fables, the fables became myths, the myths became history. It was important that people knew. It was important that the inhabitants of Earth.2 knew of the sacrifices that had been made, of the mistakes that had led to their downfall. It was important that they knew of the hardships their ancestors had undergone, of the missions of hope and the decision to journey through the collapsing wormhole and leave the survivors behind. It was important that they knew about what had come before: history, technology, religion, science, people. Humans. The very foundation upon which Earth.2 was forged. The shrines dedicated to the billions butchered by the mistakes of the past stood glistening beneath the burning ball in the sky. Carved from pink rocks at the source of the stream that gave them life, the shrines were smoothed out to resemble those of importance: Armstrong and Gowland, Artemis and Alara, Hypnos and Priapus. The lives of the Kims were chronicled and all knew what had happened. But Hera Kim was more focussed on the future. Voted as the President of Earth.2, Hera made her only sole decision: unity. Everything else could be decided by others, but Hera was adamant that unity was needed in order for humanity to survive, for their future to be definite. Just as the histories of her ancestors had been passed on, so too had the histories of Earth: the wars fought over differences. It was important to her that the same mistakes weren't made again. On Earth.2 everyone was equal and, as Hera looked out at the setting sun, she thought that maybe, just maybe, the future of the human race was possible.

Acknowledgments

First and foremost: Mam - thank you for always believing. Dad - thank you for the inspiration. David - we didn't do too bad, did we?

This collection of stories wouldn't have been possibly without my amazing band of editors and proofreaders: Katie Barton, Ryan Gamble, Barbara Harland, Steven Lauder, Conal McKenzie, Mary Picken, Alicia Skelton, Craig Wallace, Eleanor Ward and Helen Williams. I can't thank you enough.

I've written for as long as I can remember, but it wasn't until I was 18 that I first received true acknowledgement. Janice Riley, my sixth form tutor, said she was looking forward to seeing my name in print. It's taken eight years, but here it is. Thank you for everything!

Thank you to Helen Williams, my fantastic dissertation tutor who painstakingly guided me towards a First class essay, and who has supported me ever since. It was with your help that I received my first taste of being a professional writer. Your introduction to Paul Cordes, who hosted Newcastle's Photography Festival in 2014, to Mary Picken, who produced my script, and to Colin Cuthbeth, Lewis Cuthbert and Willem Evans, who gave life to my words, allowed something I never thought would happen come to fruition. Writing and staging a play was an incredibly daunting and humbling experience, and one from which I learnt an incredible amount. I can't thank you all enough.

My Masters course in Creative Writing introduced me to Andrew Crumey, Laura Fish, Michael Green, Daisy Hildyard, Fiona Shaw, Tony Williams, tutors who helped me to hone my craft. And my fellow students, who offered feedback on my work (including 'The Abyss') - thank you all: Grace Campbell, Karen Collins, Peter Dawson, Kirsty Ferry, Nikita Garner, Barbara

Harland, Debora James, Jamie Kelly, Catherine Patmore, Christal Radix, De-Ann Smith, Rebecca Summers and Margaret Wells.

Thank you to 101Words, who first published 'He' in print in 2017.

And, finally, thank you to all that has read my stories. Friends, family, strangers. I put my heart and soul into this collection. This is only the beginning.

Printed in Great Britain
by Amazon